Running for his life...

Jackson leaped into the chopper and slammed the door shut. He spun around to see the monstrosity roaring at him from behind the slab of thick Plexiglas. He saw its skin, a transparent membrane pulled taut over a huge skull, and within the black sockets below its distended brow two narrow, red, murderous eyes. Where its nose should have been was a ragged, oozing hole. The monster cocked its head as if showing off its neck wound, glared at Jackson as it thrust its twisted fangs out at the window, and began to pound the aircraft with its insectlike extremities. The craft shook, listed. The creature's pincers started to shear upward through the aluminum door.

BOOKS BY PAUL ZINDEL

THE PIGMAN
Outstanding Children's Books of 1968, *The New York Times*
Notable Children's Books, 1940–1970 (ALA)
Best of the Best for Young Adults, 1966–1988 (ALA)

MY DARLING, MY HAMBURGER
Outstanding Children's Books of 1969, *The New York Times*

I NEVER LOVED YOUR MIND
Outstanding Children's Books of 1970, *The New York Times*

THE EFFECT OF GAMMA RAYS ON MAN-IN-THE-MOON MARIGOLDS
1971 Pulitzer Prize for Drama
Best American Play of 1970
(New York Drama Desk Critics Circle Award)
Notable Books of 1971 (ALA)
Best of the Best for Young Adults 1966–1988 (ALA)

I LOVE MY MOTHER
(a picture book, illustrated by John Melo)

PARDON ME, YOU'RE STEPPING ON MY EYEBALL!
Outstanding Children's Books of 1976, *The New York Times*
Best Books for Young Adults, 1976 (ALA)

CONFESSIONS OF A TEENAGE BABOON
Best Books for Young Adults, 1977 (ALA)

THE UNDERTAKER'S GONE BANANAS

THE PIGMAN'S LEGACY
Outstanding Children's Books of 1980, *The New York Times*
Best Books for Young Adults, 1980 (ALA)

A STAR FOR THE LATECOMER
(with Bonnie Zindel)

THE GIRL WHO WANTED A BOY

HARRY AND HORTENSE AT HORMONE HIGH

TO TAKE A DARE
(with Crescent Dragonwagon)
Best Books for Young Adults, 1982 (ALA)

THE AMAZING AND DEATH-DEFYING DIARY
OF EUGENE DINGMAN
(A Charlotte Zolotow Book)
1988 Books for Teen Age (New York Public Library)

A BEGONIA FOR MISS APPLEBAUM
(A Charlotte Zolotow Book)
Best Books for Young Adults, 1989 (ALA)
1990 Books for Teen Age (New York Public Library)

THE PIGMAN & ME
(A Charlotte Zolotow Book)
Best Books for Young Adults, 1993 (ALA)
Notable Children's Books, 1993 (ALA)

DAVID & DELLA
(A Charlotte Zolotow Book)

LOCH
1995 Recommended Books for the Reluctant
Young Adult Reader (ALA)

PAUL ZINDEL

THE DOOM STONE

HYPERION PAPERBACKS FOR CHILDREN
NEW YORK

1 3 5 7 9 10 8 6 4 2

The text for this book is set in 12-point Garamond.

Library of Congress Cataloging-in-Publication Data

Zindel, Paul
The doom stone / Paul Zindel — 1st Hyperion pbk. ed.
p.   cm.
Summary: When fifteen-year-old Jackson
visits his aunt in England,
he becomes caught up in a chase to capture
an unknown creature who
is stalking and killing people on the plains
surrounding ancient Stonehenge.
ISBN 0-7868-1157-9
[1. Monsters—Fiction. 2. Stonehenge (England)—
Fiction.]
I. Title
[PZ7.Z647Do   1996]
[Fic]—dc20
96-3463

To Bill Morris

CONTENTS

THE
DOOM
STONE

~1~

THE SIGHTING

The stones and the nightmare were waiting for Jackson Cawley as the landrover raced toward the storm. Thick, twisted trunks of oak trees lined the road, their branches reaching high across like fingers of hands straining to pray.

There had already been warnings that nothing would go smoothly on this journey. Jackson's charter flight from New York had landed in London during heavy rains and violent turbulence. The Heathrow terminal was mobbed with spring break travelers, and it was past six by the time Jackson had made it through Customs and linked up with Sergeant Tillman, his ride to Salisbury.

Tillman found Jackson to be a good-looking fifteen-year-old with shaggy brown hair and intense green eyes who did nothing but ask questions: Will I be staying near Stonehenge? Are there mounds filled with ancient human bones? Did high priests perform blood sacrifices?

The stocky sergeant smiled. "I'm no expert on Stonehenge. There will be guides there who can tell you the whole history when you take a tour," he said, carrying the boy's canvas suitcase to the landrover. He opened the door on the passenger side. Jackson got in, took his suitcase, and swung it behind him to the backseat. As Sergeant Tillman slid into the driver's seat, Jackson noticed he was wearing a gun. "Are you on special assignment?" Jackson asked.

"Yes," Tillman said.

"Did you ever have to shoot anyone?"

Sergeant Tillman smiled. "Not lately." He started the landrover and drove out the airport exit. After several miles he reached the M3, and followed it for a good distance until turning onto A303 west.

It took a spectacular thunderbolt to halt Jackson's questions, which had begun to center around the landrover's two-way radio. The last of the shattered sunset slid down beneath the rim of dark, huge clouds mushroomed at the horizon. A strong wind rattled and shook the branches of green willows along a stream.

CLICK CLICK

Jackson heard the sounds. "What's going on?" he asked.

The sounds came faster, more furious.

"Hailstones," Tillman said.

Jackson had never been in a hailstorm. He watched the front of the landrover crust up with the falling ice pellets. They fell harder still, and in a few moments the road was a chalky white. The ice melted quickly.

For a long stretch the roadway cut through a forest choked by thickets and twisting, thick vines. The headlights picked up red-and-white TANK CROSSING signs and a series of wooden stakes in the earth.

"What are those?" Jackson asked.

"Markers for the military territories," the sergeant explained. "Restricted areas."

BAM

There was another crash of thunder as a crop duster biplane fled the sky and nightfall to land in a field. Here the shoulders of the road began to lift into eerie mounds, blocking the view of the countryside and making the road appear to drop into a long, open grave. Several miles later, beyond a hog farm and a sign for a gravel operation, the road rose onto a ridge with a breathtaking expanse of Salisbury Plain in front of them.

"I can take a slight detour up onto A344 if you want a closer look at Stonehenge," Sergeant Tillman said. "There's a good view of it from there."

"Great."

Tillman took a small northwestward road, then doubled back beyond a thatch-roofed farmhouse. He pointed. "Dead ahead."

Jackson strained forward against his seat belt to see through the fogging windshield. There was another flash of lightning, and his heart crawled up into his throat when he saw the circle of massive stones. Stonehenge stood like a ring of giant sentinels.

Closer, a thunderhead burst over the landrover. Suddenly Jackson could barely see the great stones between the sweeps of the worn, thumping wipers. There were no lights, no cars or tourists in the parking lot.

"Where is everybody?" Jackson asked.

"Stonehenge closes at five," Sergeant Tillman said, his foot staying heavy on the accelerator.

"Closes?" That was like being back in the States and finding out that Mount Rushmore closes or that Niagara Falls gets turned off.

The stones became framed by a sturdy chain-link fence that ran along the edge of the road. The rain was a deluge now, blurring everything. Jackson hoped for a bolt of lightning, a sharp wide crackle on the horizon, so he could see close up this monumental temple of the wind.

The flash of lightning came, and in that moment Jackson saw the true enormousness of the stones. But there was something else. Out of the corner of his eye he glimpsed a figure moving swiftly from the shadows of the stone circle and heading for the road-side fence.

Jackson wiped the window and strained to see through the night and the rain. Three lightning flashes hit one after the other like a tremendous sky strobe. It was then he could see that it was a young man in a plaid shirt with a ponytail running toward the landrover. The lightning made the man's movements unreal, as though he were a flickering image on a movie screen. The man kept coming.

In the next flash of lightning Jackson saw the young man's face twisting into a scream, his hands desperately reaching out toward the speeding landrover. Jackson's first thought was that someone was playing a joke. He was used to all sorts of scams and insanity on the streets of Manhattan—but then, behind the terrified man, he saw a shadowy form coming fast, like a jungle animal closing on its prey.

Another explosion of blue-white lightning.

Jackson saw the shadow crash into the young man, hurtling his body against the fence with such force, the hair of his ponytail burst loose to fan out like snakes on the weave of metal. The dark thing was behind the man, twisting his neck terribly, crushing the young man's face into the wire fence as the landrover flew past.

Jackson found his voice. "Stop!"

"What?" Sergeant Tillman was momentarily startled, his eyes fixed on the wet roadway ahead. "What's going on?" he asked, his tone quickly military again.

"Somebody's being attacked!" Jackson cried out, twisting in his seat to indicate behind them. "Some guy's being attacked by an animal!"

"Hold on."

Sergeant Tillman braked hard. With a single motion he spun the landrover around and crashed his foot back down on the accelerator. The tires burned rubber and finally gripped, and the landrover raced back toward the stones.

"Where?" the sergeant asked.

"There," Jackson said, pointing across the hood.

The sergeant slid the landrover to a halt on the grass-and-clay shoulder of the road. "Wait here," he ordered as he leaped out of the car with his gun drawn and ran to the fence. Jackson knew Tillman would be trained to act in emergencies, but he hadn't expected him to believe his report of an attack so quickly. Jackson jumped out of the landrover after the sergeant. The stark, raw smell of the storm socked into his nose and lungs.

"It was here," Jackson shouted against the wind, running his hand along the wire mesh as it glowed in the landrover's headlights. He looked down expecting to see the young man's body crumpled into the mud. Lightning flashed, followed by a growl of thunder.

There was no body of a young man.

No animal.

Nothing but the huge, towering stones bearing silent witness to the night.

The sergeant clipped his gun back into its holster. "Come on," he said, putting his arm around Jackson's wet shoulder and starting him back toward the land-rover. "Your aunt is waiting for us."

~2~

NIGHT SOUNDS

Sergeant Tillman made a report to his base camp on the landrover's radio before setting off toward the town of Salisbury. Jackson was too thrown by the attack on the young man to catch all of Tillman's clipped army jargon. All he understood was that a couple of military police were being dispatched from the camp to check the area around the stones.

"You and your aunt are staying at Langford's Guest House," Tillman said, turning left onto a narrow, heavily eroded street on the north fringe of town.

Jackson brushed his hair out of his eyes. "Down here?" he asked, as the landrover hit deep into a pothole. A spray of muddy water flew over the fenders.

"This is where the army puts up civilian visitors," Tillman said.

Jackson glanced at the sergeant's eyes. They were red and squinted like those of a poker player playing his cards close to his vest.

Jackson was used to secrets and unexpected events whenever it came to visiting his aunt Sarah on one of her anthropological work assignments. The summer before, she had invited him along on a fossil dig in India. They had had to sleep in hammocks at night to escape giant jungle rats that would climb into their stilted hut. His last spring break he had visited her in Ethiopia, where she had been hired by a university to help carbon-date a skull that had been nicknamed "Lucy's Sister." There he had had to wear steel-reinforced boots as a defense against leeches capable of needling into a human foot.

There was a flash of lightning and he saw his aunt—a tall, strong woman with high cheekbones and worried eyes—waiting in front of the guest house.

~

Dr. Sarah Cawley breathed a sigh of relief when she saw the landrover pull into the driveway of the dismal-looking guest house. She darted out into the headlights holding an oversized black umbrella.

"I'm sorry," she told Jackson as she opened the mud-splattered door of the landrover and leaned inside. "They called me from the camp and told me what had happened. Are you all right?"

"Sure," Jackson said. "Y-whay oes-day eargeant-

Say illman-Tay ave-hay a-ay un-gay?" he added, which he knew his aunt would understand was pig Latin for *Why does Sergeant Tillman have a gun?* Jackson's pig Latin was the most basic kind. He'd take the first letter of a word, move it to the end of the word, and then tack "ay" on it. Short words beginning with a vowel, like "is" and "in," he'd just usually add "ay" to, making them "is-ay" and "in-ay."

"Ater-lay," Dr. Cawley told him, which was pig Latin for *later*. She ran her fingers through her frosted, short-cropped hair and looked across to Tillman, who looked puzzled. She was used to Jackson trying to drive people crazy by making them think he knew a secret language. "Thanks for getting my nephew here. He's my favorite person in the world."

"I shouldn't have taken him around by the stones," Tillman said.

"Hey, I wanted to see them," Jackson defended the sergeant.

Dr. Cawley told Tillman, "Lieutenant Rath wants you to wait around for a call. Mrs. Langford's got hot soup and a sandwich in the sitting room."

"Thanks," the sergeant said.

Jackson grabbed his suitcase and got out under the umbrella with his aunt. The rain had slowed, but the wind tugged violently at the umbrella as they started back toward the house. "I called New York, but you had already left for the airport," Dr. Cawley said. "Your mother and father sounded as obsessive as ever. I lied and said the call was to thank them for letting you come visit. If you had been home, I was going to tell you not to come."

"Why?"

She rolled her eyes as they reached the shabby entrance awning. "You don't want to know." She closed the umbrella, opened the door, and they went in.

Dr. Cawley wiped her shoes on a shaggy straw mat and set the dripping umbrella into an ornate wrought-iron stand. Jackson went to the center of the foyer and started looking every which way at once. The walls were covered with gold-framed oil paintings, and there were shelves filled with antique porcelain plates and goblets. Crystal chandeliers hung from the ceiling. *It's delightful, it's de-lovely . . .* a man in a powder-blue dinner jacket was singing while playing the piano in the center hall. Jackson realized it was a restaurant with dozens of guests happily eating and drinking at tables.

"This is a great place," Jackson said. "How come it looks so weird from the outside?"

"The British army subsidizes it but wants it all kept low profile," Dr. Cawley explained. "One of the military's many little secrets around Salisbury." An archway on the right framed a bustling, charming kitchen with an Asian chef and several waitresses.

"He made it, Mrs. Langford," Dr. Cawley called to an elegant-looking woman totaling bills at a small white wicker desk.

Mrs. Langford waved. "Welcome, Jackson! We were worried about you in the storm."

Jackson waved back. He was amazed at how quickly his aunt made friends wherever she went. Even the chef gave them a smile.

Dr. Cawley led Jackson up the center staircase.

"Why does Tillman have to wait for a call?" Jackson asked.

"They're sending a helicopter for him and me."

"You're going up in a chopper tonight? In this storm?"

"It's a front moving through," Dr. Cawley said as they reached the next floor. "Weather in Salisbury is like it is in Texas: If you don't like it, wait a minute. By midnight you'll be able to see the moon and stars."

"Where's the helicopter going to land?"

"They've got a pad in the middle of a pepper patch out in the back. The army hides everything around here. There's a swimming pool in a hothouse. You'll see in the morning."

Dr. Cawley led Jackson down the hallway, past

several large detailed paintings of slaughtered ducks and grouse after a hunt, and up another flight of stairs. The dead birds reminded him of the last time his aunt had been hired in England. A 5,000-year-old mummy had been found in the elevator shaft of a London hotel. It had taken his aunt three weeks to date the mummy and trace it to a West End art dealer. Another time, Scotland Yard had called her in to identify a piece of a skull dug up near Kensington Palace. It turned out to be the remains of a pig.

"I had your supper brought upstairs to our rooms because I didn't know how late you'd be getting in. Actually what we have is more like our own private apartment. Besides, we have to talk." Dr. Cawley opened a wood-slat door at the top of the staircase. "Don't let my friend scare you," she warned as she went in.

Jackson followed her inside and she flicked on the lights.

"*Ahhh!*" Jackson cried out, freezing in his tracks.

A hideous, glaring white head, its mouth gaping wide with thick, jutting teeth, stared straight at him.

"Jeez," Jackson said, feeling adrenaline pulse through him and his face flush. It took him another second to realize it was a skull sitting on top of a telephone table.

"That's Pithecus," his aunt explained. "It's short

for *Australopithecus africanus*—one of man's earliest relatives, about three million years old. I don't think you've ever met him before."

"No."

"He's part of what we've got to talk about," she said pointedly. She took his suitcase from him and put it in the room on the left. "You've got your own room and bath in the apartment, but we share the sitting room."

Jackson looked at a long table covered with his aunt's books and sketches. Skulls and jawbones of several other prehistoric humans and primates lay on top of plastic bubble wrap and shipping crates.

"Most of these specimens came in today from my friends at the British Museum," Dr. Cawley said. She placed a chair at the table for Jackson in front of a tray containing a bowl of soup, a sandwich, and a glass of chocolate milk.

"What I saw tonight at Stonehenge has something to do with these teeth and skulls, doesn't it?" Jackson said. "That's why the army chopper's coming—to search while the trail's still hot?"

"All you have to do is rest up from the trip."

"I slept on the plane," Jackson protested. "I want to go with you on the chopper."

"Tell me what happened."

Jackson took a bite of the sandwich and chewed as he talked. He described how the young man with the ponytail ran out from the circle of stones with the shadow racing after him like a jungle animal. "What was the guy doing at Stonehenge anyway?" he asked.

"He was probably one of what I call New Age hippies," his aunt said. "Stonehenge is like their Woodstock. Some of them think it's a magical place, that they'll renew their identity and spirit there. That it's not something the government should be allowed to sell tickets for. The young man you saw could have been from the top of Scotland. There probably won't be a missing persons report on him for months."

Jackson wiped a milk mustache from his mouth and stared at Pithecus. "Aunt Sarah, why did the army hire you? What do they want with an anthropologist?"

Dr. Cawley poured herself a glass of wine and pulled a chair up next to him. "During the last few months, there have been some . . ." She hesitated. "There have been *mutilations.*"

"What kind of mutilations?"

"Local farmers found animals at first. A cow. A few sheep. They appeared to have been mauled and half eaten by some kind of large animal. Last month the number of attacks increased. As you know, I've got a lot of friends and colleagues in Britain—and when they couldn't figure it out, they told the army to call me. I listened to what they had to say, then told them to check for an escaped circus animal or someone's wild pet that had gotten too big to handle. That's what it usually turns out to be when there are killings like these. It spells large bear or big cat like a lion or tiger—none of which is, to say the least, indigenous to this countryside. The mutilations were occurring over a one-hundred-twenty-square-mile area, roughly the hunting territory needed by a mature grizzly. Last week a couple of creepy things happened that made the army decide to spend the big bucks and fly me in."

"What?"

"The animal killed a soldier, a young kid on patrol at a top-secret biochemical lab up near Alton Down. His skull was crushed. I examined the wounds with a military coroner." Dr. Cawley stood up.

She walked around the table to a specimen covered by a damp towel. "We took measurements of the neck wounds and made molds. Then I constructed a mockup of the animal's jaws from its bite."

Dr. Cawley lifted the towel.

Jackson swallowed hard.

Glistening clay jaws, thick and low slung, supported

a startling spray of immense, twisted fangs—the kind that could easily crack bone and tear raw meat.

Dr. Cawley pointed to molars behind the fangs. "These," she said, "are teeth identical to those of a hominid."

"What's a hominid?"

"A human, or a member of the human family."

Jackson stopped chewing. "You think this thing is human?"

"To be truthful," Dr. Cawley said, "at this point I don't know what to think."

The phone rang and Dr. Cawley answered it. When she hung up, she turned back to Jackson. "That was Tillman in the lobby," she said, tossing back the rest of her wine. "The helicopter's here."

~ 3 ~

THE STALKING

"You didn't say anything about bringing a kid," Lieutenant Rath snapped from the copilot seat as Tillman helped Jackson board the helicopter. Dr. Cawley pulled her raincoat tightly about herself and motioned Jackson to slide along the backseat.

"Jackson's my assistant," Dr. Cawley said, giving her nephew a wink. "Besides, he's seen what we're looking for."

Lieutenant Rath's eyes narrowed like a cat's under his puffy lids. "I thought all he saw was a shadow?"

"A *big* shadow," Jackson said.

Rath glared at Dr. Cawley, his face gaunt in the light from the chopper's control panel. "Next time check with me."

Jackson's knees squashed up against the cold of the cockpit fire extinguisher as his aunt climbed in next to him, followed by Tillman. Captain Richards, a blocky, bearded sharpshooter, sat across from

Tillman on a jump seat. They both held high-powered rifles with scopes.

"Let's go," Lieutenant Rath ordered the pilot.

The top rotor's spin made a scraping sound like metal sliding upon metal. When the full power kicked in, the roar was deafening.

"Too noisy," Dr. Cawley complained, leaning forward away from the vibrating wall of the cabin. The pilot adjusted his earphones and pencil mike.

"Use Stalk Mode," Rath commanded. The pilot reached out to the control console and hit a switch. The roar of the engines dropped into a low, whooshing sound as the chopper lifted into the air.

Jackson knew from the moment he had seen the army chopper that it was a heavily modified recon model. A searchlight, fuel pods, and exterior-mounted cameras made it look like a huge black wasp waiting on the pad behind Langford's. As his aunt had predicted, the rain had stopped and there was a near-full moon in the sky.

"We start at the stones," Lieutenant Rath told Dr. Cawley.

"All right," she said.

The helicopter had a massive center island of electronic equipment, and a sliding door that opened like a minivan's. If they spotted anything, Tillman and

Richards could open the right section of the craft and have a clear line of fire.

Dr. Cawley pointed below. "That's the Avon River. Stay low and follow it."

The pilot looked to Lieutenant Rath.

"Why the river?" Rath asked.

"We know what we're looking for kills at night," she said. "If it feeds, it'll drink. That spells river to me."

Rath nodded an okay, and the pilot traced the Avon as far as West Amesbury, then headed west. The smooth, low flight of the helicopter as it closed on Stonehenge made Jackson feel that he was flying in a dream.

The chopper slowed and hovered above the center of the circle. Tillman and Richards, clutching their rifles, slid open the door. Without a word, they took the releases off their weapons.

"It's cold," Dr. Cawley complained as the wall of night air moved into the cockpit.

Lieutenant Rath hit another switch and the island of electronic equipment leaped to life. A single large, horizontally mounted TV screen in the center lit up like a flickering wizard's table.

Rath asked Jackson, "Where did you see the attack?" He threw on the exterior searchlight and cameras. The monitor registered a bird's-eye view of the stones.

"Here," Jackson said, leaning over to point out the spot on the screen.

Rath pressed a button, and the area under Jackson's finger enlarged to fill the entire screen. "The cams have a four-hundred-to-one zoom ratio," he said. Jackson indicated where he'd seen the fleeing young man race to the fence.

"How would you know if the animal's still down there?" Jackson asked.

Rath hit another button, and the picture on the screen was replaced by amorphous colored patterns. "Thermal images," he explained. One speck looked hot, red, and moving. "That's the only thing alive." He touched the controls, and the zoom enlarged the heat image. It was that of a rodent. "If we want, we can hear it," he said. He threw a switch controlling the exterior directional mikes. A faint squeaking and scratching noise came across the interior speakers— but another series of sounds intruded.

WHIR CLICK WHIR

The heat cam refocused on the roadway several hundred feet away. The image was that of a warm engine in a parked landrover.

WHIR CLICK

The camera moved again. Appearing on the monitor was an eerie heat image of a large mammal moving on the ground toward the stones. Rath motioned the pilot to reposition the chopper, as Tillman and Richards kept their eyes glued to the sights of their rifles. A second hot image joined the first, and Rath switched the screen back to standard imaging.

"Hold your fire," Rath ordered, as he saw a pair of military police. One of the soldiers was broadcasting to the chopper pilot via a portable radio. The pilot relayed the message to Rath: "They haven't seen anything."

"Tell them to return to camp," Rath said. "We'll head west toward Warminster."

"No," Dr. Cawley said. "Too populated. Any wild animal worth its salt would head north or northeast."

Rath signaled the pilot. The chopper started north.

"We'll check Black Heath, then cross to Netheravon," Dr. Cawley elaborated, trying not to threaten Lieutenant Rath's command of the search. "The most likely hiding place during daylight would be an area once known as Savernake Forest. There's tree cover. Abandoned quarries."

The pilot looked to Rath. "She's talking forty to fifty kilometers."

"The distance works in our behalf," Dr. Cawley said. She checked her watch. "The attack was an hour ago. Whatever this carnivore is, it's still out here on the plain."

"Then we'll find it," Lieutenant Rath said, motioning the pilot on.

Clusters of mounds rose from the farmlands as the chopper continued to fly silent and low. Jackson whispered to his aunt, "Are those what I think they are?"

Dr. Cawley looked down to where Jackson was pointing. "You wanted to see burial mounds," she said, "you got burial grounds."

"Each one is filled with bodies?"

"Mostly cremated. Some have crockery and stones along with the ashes," Dr. Cawley said. "From the early Bronze Age. They were into all kinds of mass burials."

WHIR CLICK WHIR

Lieutenant Rath switched the screen back to the thermal imaging mode. A heat image made Rath sit up, alert. "Target at eleven o'clock."

"It's moving," Richards said.

Jackson laughed. "It's a cow."

Rath glared at him. "What?"

"I see a herd of cows. Looks like a couple hundred of them," Jackson said.

"He's right," the pilot confirmed.

"What we're looking for isn't around here, or these animals wouldn't be this calm," Dr. Cawley said as the screen filled with the image of the herd.

Near Black Heath they flew over several large estates edging Salisbury Plain. Toward Netheravon the countryside was planted farmland, and the light from the moon so bright that livestock could be spotted by eye. The thermal images clicked in on wildlife. There were two puzzling heat images. One turned out to be a hot spring. The second was a heated swimming pool on a horse farm.

"What's that barking?" Dr. Cawley asked as the helicopter neared the Avon at a point where it snaked below the town of Netheravon.

The pilot banked the chopper. Ahead, the fingers of a night fog crawled out of the river and reached into the plain.

Rath punched up the power of the directional mikes and locked the pilot's guide screen onto the source of the barking dog. Appearing on the monitor were the heat images of two large structures and a tract of small rectangular shapes. Rath hit the zoom.

"It's a cemetery," he said.

Jackson looked out the window. He was the first to see the two figures standing at the edge of the graveyard. One was a young girl with long straw-colored hair that fell to her waist. She looked ghostly in a white nightgown. The dog at her side was a giant shaggy Irish wolfhound barking at something down near the river. The girl looked up and waved to the chopper as it made a low pass.

"Why is that girl out there at this hour?" Dr. Cawley asked. She leaned forward to check the heat images on the screen. "What's that on the bank of the river?"

Tillman checked out his right window. "An old gristmill."

The mill appeared abandoned, with gaping holes in its thatched roof. Its waterwheel was still turning, water from the river cascading down from wide, fragmented slats.

Rath gave the pilot the signal to hover and hit a switch on the thermal imaging control.

WHIR CLICK

A heat map of the interior of the mill came up on the screen.

"You didn't tell us this thing could see through walls," Dr. Cawley said.

"It's not the kind of P.R. we want," Rath said. "Locals wouldn't care for it if they knew we could look into their bedrooms."

The scan locked onto a strong red glow.

"Set us down," Rath ordered. The pilot circled back and landed in a clearing between the mill and the girl with the barking dog.

"Keep the rotors going," Rath ordered, holding the heat scan locked on the mill.

Tillman and Richards hit the muddy ground, running toward the mill and the river with their rifles ready. Tillman carried a flashlight, keeping it trained on the path ahead. Rath went out after his men as Dr. Cawley slid across the seat toward the open door.

"That girl shouldn't be out here at this hour," Dr. Cawley said. "I'm going to tell her to go home."

Jackson said, "I'll go with you."

"No," Dr. Cawley said. "Stay here."

Dr. Cawley stepped down out of the chopper. She clasped her raincoat close about her until she was well clear of the spinning rotors, then started back through the mist toward the cemetery. Jackson was grateful to be able to stretch his legs away from the cold, rigid cylinder of the fire extinguisher. He kept one eye on the monitor as its automatic scan swept the mill section by section.

Suddenly the bright glow on the screen became a weaker one.

"It looks like there's a horizontal form near the

roof," Jackson said. Like a disgruntled creep, the pilot ignored him and began busily writing in the chopper's flight log.

Tillman and Richards reached the entrance to the mill. The front door was cracked and broken, hanging open from a single hinge. Tillman shone the light inside. Richards moved in to the bottom of a staircase. He crouched, with both hands on his gun ready to fire. Tillman followed, directing the flashlight up the stairs.

"I'm going," Richards said, then rushed up the steps three at a time. He took cover behind a crate. Tillman did a slow count to three and went up after him, freezing next to a barrel. Half of the room was a pile of broken beams and thatch that had long ago crashed in from the rotting roof.

Richards pointed to a pair of naked legs protruding beyond a web of planking and vines that had invaded near the chimney.

"Wake up!" Tillman shouted.

There was no response.

Richards took up a barrel slat from the floor and prodded the legs. "British army here!" Tillman said loudly.

Again, nothing.

Tillman rolled the barrel over next to a crate at the edge of the heap. Richards raised his rifle as Tillman climbed up. There was a slithering movement, a fat snake crawling along a wedge of dank collapsed thatch. Slowly, Tillman straightened up and swung the light onto the youthful body of a man. The young man's plaid shirt was wet and muddied, his arms and legs extended as though he had been crucified.

"What's happening?" Richards asked.

Tillman shone the light onto the figure's head. It struck the face at a sharp angle, and he saw the open mouth frozen into a death scream. There was a wound at the base of the skull, a cluster of dried blood mixed with scattered hair—hair long enough to have been easily worn in a ponytail.

Tillman knew the dead body was not the bright red glows he'd seen on the thermograph screen.

"Follow me," he told Richards, and they started down toward the grinding room.

~4~

ENCOUNTER

"I think they found a dead body," Jackson told the pilot as he watched the bright heat images of Tillman and Richards leave the weaker glow and descend to the bottom of the mill.

"Maybe yes, maybe no," the pilot muttered, continuing to write in the flight log.

Rath waited, gun drawn, at the top of the path to the mill. Jackson checked out the open door of the chopper back toward the mist-filled cemetery. He could barely see his aunt talking to the strange girl with the wolfhound.

"How come the heat scan doesn't pick up images in the river?" Jackson asked the pilot.

"Water blocks the transmission."

"Like lead blocks X rays?"

"Sort of."

WHIR CLICK

The automatic scan zeroed in on a new, bright glow far to the right of the heat images of Tillman and

Richards in the grinding room. It was a strange sliver coming from behind what looked to be a large, old water tank.

"You'd better look at this," Jackson said.

The pilot grunted, didn't look up.

CLICK

The scanner locked tighter on the heat image. It was stronger, clearer now.

Jackson had watched Rath, knew which switch controlled the zoom—and he hit it.

The image quickly enlarged, filling the screen. Jackson saw a limb, a powerful leg with a grotesquely muscular thigh. "Something's hiding behind a water tank!" he cried out. "Something big!"

The pilot turned at Jackson's shout, looked at the screen. Next to the form of the leg was the image of a flexing hand with claws. Jackson was out of the chopper, running toward Rath.

"It's down there!" Jackson shouted.

～

Tillman and Richards searched the last dark corner of the grinding room. The shriek of the turning water-wheel with its chipped axle and gear teeth cut through the air like nails being dragged across a blackboard. Over the din they heard a scuffling and a strange ticking sound.

TICK TICK

The soldiers halted, aware there was more than a dead body in the mill. Richards felt the hair on the back of his neck bristle. "What's that?"

Tillman shone the light onto the wall behind the tank. The ticking became faster, like the sounds from a Geiger counter. Puzzled, Tillman clipped the flashlight to his belt and started to circle the tank to the right. Richards moved counter to Tillman. He advanced slowly until the glow of Tillman's light stripped the shadows from behind the tank.

Richards scratched at his beard. "Where'd it go?"

TICK TICK TICK

The sounds were above them now.

They glanced up slowly. There were fresh scrapings on a rusted metal ladder at the side of the water tank.

"It's gone up," Tillman said.

"Yeah," Richards agreed. He slung his rifle over his shoulder, unclipped the revolver from his belt, and began climbing the ladder. Tillman stepped back, lifting the light beam up to the rim of the tank.

Richards groaned, wiping his hands as he grasped rung after rung of the ladder.

"What?"

"Slime. Stinking slime."

Richards braced against each rung for balance.

Near the top he drew himself into a crouch, then lifted his head above the rim.

"What is it?" Tillman asked.

Richards stared down at the surface of the stagnant water, its putrid smell burning in his nostrils. "I need more light."

Tillman moved back, bouncing the light off the ceiling.

"Nothing," Richards said.

"You sure?"

Richards leaned over the rim of the tank, trying to see below the surface of the foul water. He laughed. "Only a polar bear would stay underwater—"

The eruption came quickly. Richards saw a shimmering bulk flying up through his own reflected image. The living mass rose at him like a battering ram, hitting into him before his brain could think to pull the trigger of his gun. In the next split second he glimpsed an enormous skull-like face with horrifying, deep, huge eye sockets. The impact ripped his legs from the ladder and hurled his body against the ceiling beams. He was aware of being turned by great clawed hands locked on him like pincers, and he was ashamed to find himself screaming. He stared helplessly down into the skull face, saw it open its mouth. A huge, gnashing spray of twisted, razor-sharp fangs spiraled upward and began to penetrate his throat. He felt a deep unspeakable pain, saw the burst of his own blood in front of him. In his last conscious moment on earth, he knew he was being devoured alive.

At Richards' first scream, Tillman had backed away, trying to get a clear shot at the ungodly nightmare rising from the tank. He saw the monster twisting, turning Richards' body as though deliberately using it as a shield. The creature began biting with the power and speed of instinct until Richards' severed head fell down at Tillman's feet with a sickening thud.

CRAAACK

The side of the tank exploded. The beast and a wall of water flew at Tillman. He leaped out of the path of the creature, but the slats of the tank and the surge of water smashed him with the force of an ocean wave. He staggered to his feet in the midst of the blood and debris as the monster fled out the open door.

Jackson heard the creature's sounds before he saw it coming up the path heading straight for Rath. He backed toward the helicopter as Rath fired his pistol. A single shot passed through the creature's neck, but it didn't even slow it. With a swing from its powerful arms, it sent Rath flying against a tree, then kept coming straight for Jackson.

"Yow!" Jackson cried out as he turned and ran for the open door of the chopper, the beast fast on his heels. The engines were still running. He saw the look of terror on the pilot's face, heard the chilling sounds of the beast gaining on him.

"Hurry!" the pilot shouted.

Jackson leaped into the chopper and slammed the door shut. He spun around to see the monstrosity roaring at him from behind the slab of thick Plexiglas. He saw its skin, a transparent membrane pulled taut over a huge skull, and within the black sockets below its distended brow two narrow, red, murderous eyes. Where its nose should have been was a ragged, oozing hole. The monster cocked its head as if showing off its neck wound, glared at Jackson as it thrust its twisted fangs out at the window, and began to pound the aircraft with its insectlike extremities. The craft shook, listed. The creature's pincers started to shear upward through the aluminum door.

"Hold on," the pilot shouted, thrusting the main throttle forward.

The engines roared, kicking the rotors into high speed. Now the monster screamed with rage, looked upward to the large, coughing dual exhausts atop the chopper as the thrust of the rotors neared liftoff. The beast retracted its claws, cocked its shining, deformed head again, and sniffed at something in the night air. It started away from the chopper.

"No!" Jackson cried out, knowing where the creature was heading. He looked for a wrench, a piece of pipe, anything for a weapon. He grabbed the fire extinguisher as he flung the door of the chopper open.

"Stay inside!" the pilot shouted.

"My aunt . . ." was all Jackson could gasp before he was out into the fog and running after the beast.

~

Dr. Cawley had stayed much too long talking with the young girl—whose name, she had found out, was Alma. She was picking the girl's brain about her living with her father at the cemetery and the strange sounds she had heard all week. It was the ticking sounds that had awakened her in her bed, drawn her out among the tombstones into the moonlight.

Dr. Cawley was walking her toward a brick building landscaped with manicured rhododendrons and evergreens when the shots rang out.

"Who's shooting?" the girl asked.

"Quick! Go inside!" Dr. Cawley ordered, turning her away.

The girl called her dog. The wolfhound was barking again, holding its ground like a hunting dog locked on game. Dr. Cawley heard Rath's cry and the surge of power to the chopper's engines. She was afraid for her nephew—not certain at all about what was happening. The girl took the dog by its collar, hurried to lead it away.

Sounds came out of the fog, a type of profound growling, deep and pulsing, then quickening as if a wild beast were smelling blood. Dr. Cawley saw the monstrous form coming toward them. At first she believed she was looking down an impossible corridor of time as the vision of rage loped toward her.

"Run!" she screamed at the girl with the dog.

Dr. Cawley ran from the gravestones out into the open plain, hoping she could at least draw it away long enough for the others to be safe. It was then she saw Jackson coming fast behind the creature. Jackson was alive.

"Aunt Sarah!" Jackson shouted.

"Stay away!" she screamed to Jackson as she fled from the monster. But she was out of breath, and it closed on her quickly. In a moment its teeth were digging into the back of her neck, a powerful grip near the base of her skull. She was aware of being lifted from the ground like a lion cub seized by its mother.

Then she heard another, more familiar growl.

A bulk of shaggy darkness flew out of the mist

and leaped through the air snapping, making rapid bites about the creature's legs and groin. The attack of the girl's wolfhound was violent enough to hurt and confuse the monster. It dropped Dr. Cawley as it turned to hit the dog, sending it yelping and rolling across the mud.

Dr. Cawley saw Jackson red faced, his trembling hands holding the fire extinguisher. She screamed as the beast spun toward him, at the same time that Jackson yanked the release pin and squeezed. A shrieking spray of white, blinding chemicals blasted out of its nozzle and into the eyes of the enraged skull face. The creature wiped at its eyes with the rapid motions of a huge mantis.

CRAAACK!

A gunshot.

Dr. Cawley saw the bullet tear into the creature's left shoulder. A slab of skin lifted from its body and a clear fluid burst from the wound. The creature turned, shrieked, and loped off into the night fog as Tillman ran toward them firing.

~ 5 ~

TOYS

Jackson and Tillman managed to place a dry tarpaulin underneath Dr. Cawley, trying to keep her comfortable until the army medics could arrive. The adrenaline was still pumping in Jackson's blood as he rolled up his jacket and stooped to gently place it under his aunt's head.

"I saw the wound in the creature's neck," Jackson told Tillman. "At the chopper it looked deep and pretty bad, like it should have stopped it. Then I saw it again, and it looked like it had healed—like it was healing fast!"

Tillman said, "It took my shot to its shoulder like I'd hit it with a peashooter."

The young girl with the long blond hair, her hands still trembling, brought out a blanket from the brick building.

"Thank you, Alma," Dr. Cawley told the girl as Alma tucked the blanket around her.

"I'd heard the ticking sounds," the girl said, her

voice strained. "God! I never knew it was anything so horrible!" She looked to Jackson, then stepped back holding the leash of her dog tight.

"The teeth marks are deep," the sergeant said, working on Dr. Cawley's neck wound with a first aid kit from the chopper.

"Is Richards dead?" Dr. Cawley asked.

Tillman didn't answer.

The pilot had radioed the Mayday to the camp. Two massive troop helicopters descended from the sky and landed. A portable generator was set up, and its power delivered to several racks of amber field lights. Quickly, Lieutenant Rath appointed a crew to continue the air search. A green-and-brown army research van and an ambulance with its two-note siren braying pulled into the oval drive of the cemetery.

A doctor in fatigues knelt beside Dr. Cawley. He took out a stethoscope and checked her vital signs and the condition of the neck wound. "Everything looks and sounds good," Dr. Halperin said, "but you're going to need tetanus and rabies shots. You're mainly in shock."

"Look, all I need is to get home and have a good shot of scotch," Dr. Cawley said.

The doctor took her hand. "I'm afraid that's going

to have to be a scotch after the X rays and CAT scan to make sure there are no fractures," he said. "We have to take you to Bristol. Kings Hospital." He signaled the pair of attendants who stood by the ambulance. They brought out a collapsible gurney and lifted Dr. Cawley onto it. She grabbed the doctor's sleeve. "How long am I going to be in the hospital, and don't blow hot air up my skirt!"

"One or two days."

"I'm going with you," Jackson said.

Dr. Cawley thought a moment as the attendants tightened the safety straps around her. "No, Jackson," she said. "It's better if Sergeant Tillman takes you back to the guest house. You catch some sleep. I'm going to need a few of my things—a robe, nightgown, toothbrush, and my slippers. Pack a bag for me. Tillman will deliver it to the hospital."

"You're going to need me," Jackson said. "You don't like shots."

"I'm okay," Dr. Cawley insisted. "You think it's better if you go back to New York?"

"No," Jackson answered quickly.

The attendants clicked the gurney wheels into position and began to roll Dr. Cawley past the gravestones, toward the ambulance. Jackson walked along beside her. Dr. Cawley motioned him closer to her.

"They're going to try to contain this. Don't let anyone go through my things," she whispered.

A large van pulled up, and a trio of handlers got out with bloodhounds. Jackson turned to see Alma holding back her dog at the entrance to the brick building. Dr. Cawley noticed where Jackson was looking.

"Alma's nervous—but very pretty," Dr. Cawley said, as the attendants lifted her gurney up into the ambulance.

Jackson laughed.

Lieutenant Rath's braying cut over the din of the bloodhounds as he led the handlers to where Dr. Cawley had been attacked. The dogs spun in tight circles for a few moments, sniffing at the ground. Suddenly they shuddered, strained at their leashes. A baleful howling soared from their throats, and a group of armed soldiers with high-powered rifles joined the handlers. The search team fanned out north onto the plain.

"Mrs. Langford's very reliable. She'll watch out for you," Dr. Cawley said, as the attendants climbed in the rear doors of the ambulance. "There's a lot of things to do in town—and you'll be safe. Remember, don't let anyone . . ." She noticed the attendants listening carefully to her every word, and decided to finish her sentence in pig Latin: "ear-nay y-may ork-way."

"Ight-ray," Jackson said, enjoying the puzzled look on the attendants' faces.

The doors were locked, and the driver started the ambulance. It lurched forward into the fog with its siren sounding, and his aunt was gone.

Jackson walked over to the building where Alma stood with the huge wolfhound, who began wagging his tail like a whip and sniffing at Jackson from head to toe.

"Stop that, Coffin," Alma scolded the dog.

"Coffin?"

She shrugged her shoulders. "My father's sense of humor. That beast tonight looked as if it could have put us all into coffins."

Jackson petted the dog's massive gray hairy head. "You came through for us tonight, fellah," he told the dog. "You live here?" he asked Alma.

"With my dad." She noticed him staring at her. "Why does that horrible thing . . . ?" she started to say, but then remembered she was wearing her nightgown. There was mud splattered on it, and she knew her hair had to look like it had been struck by lightning.

"In this cemetery?" Jackson asked.

Her voice cracked, but she decided to get the worst facts over with first. "My dad's the gravedigger.

The owner of the cemetery lets us live rent free in a flat above the crematorium."

Jackson stood up. Her eyes were riveted on him, watching for his reaction.

"Cool," he said.

She shuddered. "You think living at a crematorium is *cool*?"

"Sure," he said, leaning against the brick building. "I've always wanted to visit a crematorium. What's it like?"

"Have you ever been to a Chirping Chicken takeout restaurant?"

"Sure."

"It's got a big grill like that. I think the crematorium's the main reason that horror comes around here."

"You've seen Skull Face before?"

"I've heard the ticking sound. I thought it was some kind of insect or bird. Sometimes it sounds robotic. I heard it around here and at Stonehenge."

"How would you hear it there?"

"I used to work weekends at the Stonehenge souvenir shop. Most of the kids around here work there at one time or another."

"Skull Face attacked somebody at Stonehenge tonight," Jackson told her. "I think they found his body in the rafters of the mill."

Alma looked away. She'd felt enough dread for the night.

Sergeant Tillman came toward them. Coffin started barking at him. Alma tightened the grip on his leash. "You'd better go inside now, young lady," Tillman said.

"All right," Alma said. The mask of fright on her face faded enough for her to smile at Jackson. "Nice meeting you."

Jackson said, "See you."

She went inside just as several landrovers and trucks with military personnel arrived. A squad of soldiers began to lay down and secure thin sheets of plastic, as a pair of shiny black body bags was carried up the mill path toward a military coroner's van.

~

Sergeant Tillman commandeered a landrover to get Jackson back to Langford's. Tillman waited until they turned down the narrow, potholed street that led to the guest house before he said what he had to. "What happened tonight," he told Jackson, "is classified information until I notify you otherwise."

"The army doesn't want me to tell anyone we were almost killed," Jackson said, "because it might frighten the horses."

"We'll have it taken care of by dawn."

"How are you going to take care of a monster that heals bullet wounds in a minute?"

"You're not to discuss this."

"Don't forget that creature bit my aunt," Jackson went on, noticing the growing sweat stains on Tillman's shirt. "If you find it, you can check it for rabies."

Sergeant Tillman didn't answer.

So much for Mr. Nice Guy.

Tillman pulled the landrover to a halt near the overhang of the guest house. He got out and followed Jackson inside.

"I'll be down in a minute," Jackson said quickly as they entered the foyer. Tillman hesitated. He looked as if he were going to follow Jackson upstairs. Mrs. Langford appeared in a bathrobe at the top of the stairs. "Something wrong?"

"Dr. Cawley was bitten by a badger," Tillman lied loudly and clearly. "She'll be staying the night at Kings Hospital in Bristol."

"Oh, I'm sorry," Mrs. Langford said. Jackson passed her and headed for his aunt's apartment. She sounded disbelieving, as if she were accustomed to weighing all information she received from the military. "Is she in much pain?"

"No," Tillman said. "She'll be fine."

Jackson continued down the hallway past the

paintings of dead game and up the narrow staircase to the wood-slat door. He went in, turned on the light. Pithecus and the other fossils were waiting for him. Quickly, he packed his aunt's things into a small paisley suitcase. Before he zippered it up, he noticed a portable two-way radio on the table. It wasn't much larger than a walkie-talkie, and had the number 101 crudely marked on it. He tossed it in and brought the bag downstairs.

"Mrs. Langford will call me if you need anything," Tillman said.

"Thanks for the lift back."

Tillman searched for something else to say. "You have a good night," he finally settled on.

Oh, sure, Jackson thought as he turned and headed back up. In the apartment he found several more of his aunt's sketches and manuscript notes about the local henges and earthworks. Next to them he noticed a tattered, leather-bound book with legends and elaborate engravings of the stones. He took the book into his room, got undressed, and crawled under the lumpy goosedown comforter on his bed.

For a long time he lay awake propped up on pillows. The pale, gnarled body of the monster loped after him in his mind. Its hideous face was at the chopper window, the nauseating, glistening membrane taut over its huge skull. Above all, Jackson remembered the long, twisted fangs.

He tried to lose himself in the old book reading about how Stonehenge was a kind of crude observatory. That it was religious, ritual, or astronomical depending upon whom one talked to. Virgins were believed to have been dragged over the ground there to guarantee the farmers a good harvest. The book told of earth-mystery researchers who believed Stonehenge to be the center of a supernatural grid used to influence everything from crop circles to spaceship landings. It told of some people's belief that spirits pass through Stonehenge to worlds beyond— and that the stones themselves create a magnetic field that can cure bone diseases.

Finally, Jackson put the book down and turned out the lights.

The moon scattered shadows through the lace curtains. A loneliness flowed into him as he thought of his own room back in New York. There was no way he could let his parents know what had happened. They'd have him on the next plane out of there. There had been crawly creatures and things that go bump in the night on his other trips, but he and his aunt Sarah had always been together at the end of the day.

The monster is probably half human, half something else, he told himself.

He knew he mustn't think about that or he'd never get to sleep. Rather, he would think about the strange girl with the long blond hair.

～

Jackson slept until eleven the next morning. He took a shower, got dressed, and went downstairs.

"Good morning, sleepyhead," Mrs. Langford said as she was setting up the dining room for lunch. "Your aunt called."

"Is she okay?"

"She's fine. She said I should let you sleep late and save a full English breakfast for you. Mixed grill, fried eggs, tea, and toast." Mrs. Langford led him to a side buffet with electric warmers. "She didn't know if you liked hot cocoa with double cream, but I made you some anyway."

"Thanks," Jackson said, taking a plate for the food.

"Your aunt sounded chipper. They've already started the antirabies shots, and they've got her down for X rays and other tests. She wants you to call her toward dinner."

The chef and two of his kitchen workers arrived while Jackson sat at a window table eating his breakfast.

They smiled at him and began peeling red potatoes and dropping them into a large metal colander.

CLANK CLANK

Mrs. Langford took a key from her wicker desk and brought it to Jackson as he was buttering the last piece of bread from a silver toast caddy. "You know, Jackson," she said, "my son works in Liverpool now, but a lot of his old toys are in the garage out back. You're welcome to play with them, if you like."

"Toys?"

"Well, that's what I call them. Of course, my son used to treat them as if they were treasures."

Mrs. Langford took a framed photo off the piano and showed it to Jackson. A tall young man in a cap and gown was mugging for the camera. "Brian graduated from Cambridge last term, but he spent two semesters taking summer courses at U.C.L.A. His last summer he shipped back a dune buggy. All the girls in Salisbury thought it was brilliant. Do you know how to drive?"

"Sure," Jackson said. "My aunt taught me on the sly in Borneo. Are you saying I can borrow the buggy?"

"Good heavens, yes. It's a silly-looking thing— not a proper car—but you might enjoy running round the back roads and fields."

Jackson got up from the table, almost knocking his chair over.

"Brian's left all sorts of junk out there you're welcome to use," Mrs. Langford added, setting the frame back on the piano. "Lots of army surplus whatchamacallits he used to collect. He was always a pack rat."

"Thanks," Jackson said, giving his mouth a last wipe with a napkin. "The breakfast was great." He took the key and bolted out the side door.

Mrs. Langford watched from the window as he ran down the driveway. "He's a nice boy," she told the chef.

Jackson's sneakers made loud, crunching sounds on the gravel as he headed across the rear parking area. There were carports with spaces for a dozen cars. Farther back was the hothouse. The steam from the indoor heated pool fogged the hothouse windows. Beyond a vegetable garden was an old garage. Jackson unlocked the door and opened it wide.

"Yes!" Jackson cried out at the sight of the dune buggy. Its chassis was like that of a Harley Davidson motorcycle, with a handlebar throttle and tandem seats. Four "Bigfoot" tires gave it plenty of height for all terrain.

Jackson slid between the buggy and a row of shelves cluttered with old motors and all sorts of army surplus junk. He swung up into the driver's seat. The buggy had a magneto start system and a four-speed gear shift.

"KEE-YIIII!" Jackson shouted, as he threw his full weight down onto the start pedal. The motor coughed, then died, and he opened the choke. On the third kick the engine roared to life, and he straddled the seat as if he were riding a motorcycle. He threw it into first, and the buggy shot too fast out of the garage. He managed to turn before it could fly into the vegetable garden. Soon he was hurtling out into the fields behind the guest house and heading fast up a steep grassy knoll.

At the top of the hill he could see for miles around. Straight ahead was a maze of fields and fences surrounding the ruins of an old castle. The massive tower and spire of Salisbury Cathedral rose high over the town to the south. He had thought about sightseeing around the town, but now that he had wheels, he looked north. There he could see the homes and fences giving way to the open Salisbury Plain. He knew there'd be dirt paths and stretches where he could open the buggy up. Besides, he told himself, he would see Stonehenge again.

And the girl.

~6~

ALMA

Alma McPhee woke up from a dream about the American boy. She'd hardly been able to sleep all night with the loud baying of the hounds and the noisy helicopters coming and going. She washed her hair and put on her favorite ripped jeans and a funky knit sweater she'd bought at a flea market in Salisbury. She told herself not to weave any elaborate fantasies about the good-looking boy with the rowdy brown hair and dark-green eyes. When it came to making friends, Alma knew even the boys at school didn't hang around very long after they learned that her father was a gravedigger.

She looked out the window. Her father was chatting with a lieutenant while bands of soldiers still combed the grounds.

"Dad, I made you a cucumber-and-tuna-fish sandwich for lunch," she called to him. "It's in the fridge."

"Thanks, darlin'," Mr. McPhee called back.

Any of the boys who hadn't been turned off by Alma's father being a gravedigger would stop calling when they found out that a date with her meant picking her up at the caretaker's apartment in the crematorium. The flat was ordinary enough, but even her mother had long ago fled to Brighton to live with her sister.

"I don't think gravediggin's all that bad," her father had told her mother. "It's honest wages."

"I draws the line at livin' in a crematorium, I do," Mrs. McPhee had let them both know before she left. "And I don't think it's me that's the oddball round here."

Alma knew her mother had stopped loving her father a long time before they had moved from Salisbury and out to the cemetery.

"He's got a good heart," Alma would defend her dad, trying to remind her mom about his good points.

"He's as much fun as a funeral" was the last thing her mother told Alma before boarding the bus for Brighton. Alma would have gone with her, but she knew her dad needed her more. Besides, Alma had no intention of leaving for anywhere until she graduated from her school in Salisbury.

~

Jackson ran the dune buggy along the back dirt roads as far as Amesbury, then had to skirt the Ministry of Defense and private land fences that cut the landscape into vast wedges of training grounds and farms. There was a crisscrossing of dirt paths and easements that allowed him to keep moving north. He knew if he followed the Avon, he'd reach the graveyard.

Edging a tract of military land, he got the dune buggy up to its top speed near thirty miles an hour. The oversized tires kicked up a dust trail as he saw the main cluster of pines marking the cemetery. A guard in a landrover peeled away from the army encampment and headed out to intercept him.

"Hold it!" the guard ordered. He blew a shrill silver whistle, and Jackson brought the buggy to a halt.

"This is a restricted area," the guard said, pulling the landrover up next to him. "Turn back."

Alma and the wolfhound were on the steps of the crematorium. She put her hand up to her forehead to shield her eyes from the sun as she looked out onto the plain. A smile broke across her face at the sight of Jackson.

"She's a friend of mine," Jackson told the guard, pointing. Soldiers were carrying boxes out of the crematorium and loading them into a truck. "What's going on?"

"The family's moving," the guard said.

Jackson played dumb. "Why?"

"A gas leak in the area," the soldier lied. Alma started running toward them with Coffin at her side. "All right," he told Jackson, checking the thick treads on the Bigfoot tires. "But don't come in any closer with this vehicle."

"Okay," Jackson agreed.

The soldier turned the landrover and headed back as Alma reached the buggy.

"Hi," she said, out of breath. "What are you doing back here?"

Jackson smiled as he climbed down from the driver's seat. "Returning to the scene of the crime. Did they catch Skull Face yet?"

"I don't think so," she said, tossing her hair so it all fell to one side of her face. "It's still pretty spooky round here." Coffin began wagging his big tail and sniffing at Jackson's legs. "How's your aunt doing?"

"Fine," Jackson said. Coffin rolled over onto his back and starting pawing at the air with his legs. Jackson stooped to scratch the dog's chest.

She reached out and touched the handlebars of the dune buggy. "Where'd you get this?"

"Borrowed it," Jackson said. "The son of the lady

where I'm staying was a California freak. He brought back his own dune buggy."

"I remember seeing it running round Salisbury." Alma slipped a thin flash camera out of her jeans pocket. "Can I take a picture of you with it?"

"Sure."

She checked over her shoulder to make certain none of the soldiers were watching, then quickly clicked the shutter.

"I used to be into photography," Jackson said. "I was president of the junior high school photography club."

Alma said, "The only club at school I joined was chorus, but I've been taking pictures. Shots of the body bags. Bloodhounds swarming over the cemetery. I don't want the army pulling some coverup next week and saying what happened to us last night didn't happen."

"Right," Jackson said. "When anything spooky happens back home, they usually say it's a weather balloon." He glanced back toward the crematorium. Soldiers were carrying out armfuls of clothes on hangers.

"They think the monster might come back," Alma said, "so they're putting us up in the close at Salisbury Cathedral. My father used to be a gardener there."

"What's the close?"

"That's what they call the walled area around a cathedral. In Salisbury it's mainly the bishop's palace, a lot of museums, and a cloister. There's a few houses where they've been boarding glaziers and masons. There's been a lot of construction going on."

"At least you'll be safe."

"I guess so." Alma put her camera back into her pocket. "The search troops are looking north. I told the officers about hearing its *tick tick* on other nights. I think it's smart and doubles back in the river to cover its tracks."

Coffin slapped his two front paws up onto Jackson's shoulders and started licking his neck.

"Down, Coffin! Down!" Alma scolded.

Jackson let out a mock growl in Coffin's face. The dog cocked his head left, then right.

"Only kidding, fellah," Jackson said. Coffin began sniffing at his chin.

"I want to check out Stonehenge," Jackson told Alma. "Maybe that's where Skull Face's lair is. If the army captures it, they can test that weird slime it has for blood. Maybe save my aunt from having to get the whole series of rabies shots. You feel like taking a ride?"

Jackson ducked out from under the dog's paws, grabbed a stick off the ground, and threw it. Coffin took off after it.

For a moment Alma's thoughts shot back to the sight of the beast coming out of the fog. She didn't want Jackson to know she wasn't a very brave person.

"Okay," she said. "I have to tell my dad I'll meet him in Salisbury."

"Great."

She started to jog back toward the crematorium.

"Hey," Jackson called after her, "maybe you'd better bring your camera along just in case."

She shouted back, "And *Coffin*!"

~

Dr. Cawley knew that the time it took for rabies victims to go mad and die depended upon where on their body they'd been bitten. The bite she'd received at the base of her skull was the most dangerous kind, because the virus would have little distance to go to reach her brain.

"There's no question the bite contained some of the creature's saliva," Dr. Halperin told her at Kings Hospital. "Whether or not the creature's infected we don't know—but we'll begin the series of antirabies shots immediately. I've made the arrangements for you to have private accommodations."

Dr. Cawley had trouble sleeping that night in her sterile room on the ninth floor of the hospital. A second bed, empty, sat like a draped coffin next to the window. The monster's existence was still too staggering for her to make sense of.

She had long ago learned that she needed to label a phenomenon in order to be able to think about it effectively. *"Ramid,"* she said aloud to hear the sound of the label she would give to this creature. Ramid was the word for "root" in the Afar language. For several hours she lay awake, disturbed by the notoriety the event could bring her. Finally, her nerves completely shot, her eyes closed and she managed to fall asleep.

~

The next morning a young Pakistani attendant came to take Dr. Cawley down for her CAT scan. "I'm Muhammad," the attendant introduced himself.

It was in the elevator as Muhammad took her down to the radiology department that Dr. Cawley felt a pronounced difference in her thinking process. She was replaying the checklist in her head: keep after Rath for the results of the bio lab tests on the beast's fluid samples; Ramid had a short muzzle, clearly qualified as a vertebrate, mammal, and primate; Ramid was tailless, with an opposable thumb and shoulder blades at the back; Ramid, from the clay jaw mock-up, would more than likely have a Y shape on the surface of its molars—further defining it as a hominid; Ramid was probably a single mutant arisen full-blown because of genes run amok, or else human evolution itself had long ago taken a second, most terrible and frightening route. . . .

It was at that moment she felt her mind stumble, as though someone had hit the Delete key of her brain.

Muhammad noticed Dr. Cawley's mouth twist into a grimace. "Is something wrong?" he asked.

"No," Dr. Cawley said. She preferred to believe the strangeness that was coming over her brain, the sensation that her mind was being wrapped in cellophane, was due to nerves and a lack of sleep.

Outside the X-ray lab a radiologist took over from Muhammad and gave Dr. Cawley two glasses of a chalky, thick liquid to drink.

"It's got a radioactive tracer that will read on the CAT scan," the radiologist explained.

"It's bitter. Can't you put a shot of vodka in it?" Dr. Cawley asked with a wink.

The radiologist smiled, gave Dr. Cawley's hand a reassuring squeeze. Twenty minutes later he wheeled her into the main room of the radiology lab.

Dr. Cawley gazed at the massive gray machine towering above her and smelled the sharp, heavy, sickening odor of ozone. "It looks like a cyclotron."

"Yes, it's quite a monster," the radiologist agreed as he transferred her gently from the gurney onto a mechanized stainless steel sled.

"It's cold," Dr. Cawley complained, trying to keep her hospital gown tucked completely under her.

"We have to strap you in so the imaging system will read accurately," the radiologist explained. "We'll want as little motion as possible while you're inside the machine."

"How long will it take?"

"About twenty minutes."

Dr. Cawley tried to take her mind off the fact that she was going to be inserted into the center of a gigantic machine. She had told the army to look north, that Ramid would hide in forests and quarries by day. Now that she'd seen the creature, she realized from its deep-set red eyes and translucent skin that it had most likely evolved without pigment in a place far below the ground. The ancient Savernake quarries weren't deep or dark enough. There had to be another black, hidden place, a world of caves and caverns somewhere far beneath Salisbury Plain itself. It would be a labyrinth where life could evolve in endless night and without interruption.

"Hold still now," the radiologist instructed, as he

withdrew to stand behind an immense shield at the far end of the lab. He pressed a button and Dr. Cawley's body began to inch forward. She noticed slits on the metal arch above her face: DO NOT LOOK DIRECTLY INTO LASER APERTURES.

In the next few moments she believed she could feel the radioactive cocktail moving through her. She felt a tingling sensation creeping from the bite on her neck toward the center of her brain.

BUZZZZZ

The machine made a vibrating, low noise as her body was drawn slowly inside. She forced herself to keep thinking. She would call upon calm logic to keep her fears in check. There must be undiscovered dark caves. There will be Ramid and. . . .

Her mind stumbled again as though a dark veil were dropped over it. She didn't know how long it was before her next thought arrived. She wanted to scream it before it disappeared. *There would be others of its kind.* She struggled, trying to make her lips form the words. She wanted to shout out a warning from inside the machine, but some power was taking control of her brain—a bridle cutting into her mind.

~7~

THE DESCENT

Alma sat behind Jackson on the dune buggy, her hands clasped tightly around his waist.

"What kind of songs did you sing in your school's chorus?"

Alma laughed. "A lot of Irish ones. Most of the music department was Irish, so it'd be a lot of 'When Irish Eyes Are Smiling,' and that sort of thing."

She helped Jackson with the route, keeping them clear of the Ministry of Defense lands and tank crossings. Coffin kept pace off to one side as they raced toward the stones.

"Why do you think Skull Face dragged the body of the young guy all the way from Stonehenge to the old mill?" Jackson asked.

Alma pointed to a series of mounds in the middle of a farmer's wheat field. "I think it's got something to do with those," she shouted as the wind snapped her hair behind her.

"The burrows?"

"They're mainly piles of buried bones and cremated bodies. Lots of stones, too. Five thousand years ago that's what everyone wanted—to be roasted and stuck in a mound with everyone else."

"You think the beast is attracted to cremations?"

"Yes—something besides snacking."

Jackson said, "Unless it's like the cremations in India my aunt told me about. Everything doesn't end up as ashes there. Sometimes there are bits and pieces left over to float down the Ganges River."

"I think this has something to do with life and death, all right," Alma agreed. "That creature looks like it's been around a long time, like it's the local Minotaur—something prehistoric. Cremation's one of the things they did around Stonehenge. I think this monster thinks the crematorium is part of some old ritual—something for some reason it keeps an eye on."

The buggy climbed fast up the small ridge of a dirt road edging private land. At the top Jackson and Alma saw Stonehenge rising from the line of the horizon. Jackson's eye was drawn to the tallest stones standing in the middle and capped by horizontal stones.

"We'd better not go any closer or the guards will come after us for trespassing," Alma warned. "Everybody's supposed to enter across the roadway—buy tickets and walk through the tunnel. They don't know my shortcuts."

Jackson shut off the engine and set the emergency brake. In the distance the crowd of regular tourists looked like ants milling about on the path circling the stones.

Jackson helped Alma down from the buggy. They walked through tall grass, keeping far from the crowd and the stones.

Jackson threw a stick and Coffin took off after it.

"There are flint mines around here, and more cremation holes," Alma said. "They've plugged most of them up with cement, but I wouldn't put it past Skull Face to pop up out of one."

"What do they say about Stonehenge on the tour?"

"How the stones got here. The smaller, blue stones were brought down from the Preseli Mountains in southwest Wales. The giant sarsen stones were dragged over forty kilometers from Marlborough Downs to the north. Most of the weird things I know I've gotten from the cathedral library. They've got the really old books with the freakiest theories about Stonehenge."

Jackson sat down cross-legged and looked toward the stones. "All I ever learned in school about Stonehenge was that it had something to do with knowing when the longest day of the year was."

Alma sat on the grass next to him. "If you stand at the center of the circle, you can tell it's the summer solstice if the sun rises over a stone called the Hell Stone."

"The Hell Stone?"

Alma broke off a daisy stalk and chewed on the end of it. "Other people call it the Friar's Heel Stone. You can understand both of its names if you believe the legend that says it was the Devil who put the stones here. The Devil boasted that no human would ever be able to figure out how all these stones got there. But a friar saw what happened and threatened to tell the secret, so the Devil threw the Hell Stone on him and crushed him to death."

"Where did you hear Skull Face?" Jackson asked.

"Around here," Alma said, breaking off the stalk of another daisy.

"Right where we're sitting?"

"Close."

Jackson got up and brushed himself off. He put out his hand. Alma took it, and he pulled her to her feet. They headed back to the buggy with Coffin racing ahead of them.

"Where are we going?" Alma asked.

"Show me *exactly* where you heard Skull Face."

Jackson climbed back up onto the driver's seat. He gave a single slam downward on the kick-start pedal, and the motor roared. He swung Alma back up onto the seat behind him and shifted into first.

Alma pointed with her right hand in front of him. "This way."

Jackson kept the buggy far from the tourists and stones. Ditches and slabs of ground overlapped each other. His foot hit the accelerator too hard and the buggy took off at a sharp angle, then landed front wheels first. The back tires sank into a deep hollow of overgrown thistle and ragweed.

"What's that?" Alma asked, pointing to a fissure in the side of the hollow.

Jackson shut off the engine and got down from the buggy for a closer inspection of the hole. He lay on his stomach to look inside. "Hey, it's a cave."

"Probably one of the old flint mines," Alma said. "We should get out of here."

Coffin shoved his head in front of Jackson to sniff around the outside of the hole.

"No, Coffin," Alma scolded, getting off the buggy and putting the leash on him. She held him back while Jackson wiggled his upper torso into the hole. A distance in front of him, he could see a rusted steel door, open. He felt a rush of wind, which made a sound like the whistle of a copper teapot starting to boil.

"Check the buggy," Jackson said. "Maybe there's a flashlight."

Alma looped the end of Coffin's leash over the tip of the front bumper and walked around the buggy. She spotted a hinge behind the rear seat. "I found something," she called to Jackson. She tugged until the top of the seat lifted up. "It's a storage compartment with junk," she said, looking inside.

"What kind of junk?"

"A few spanners and something that looks like a stick of dynamite."

"A road flare!" Jackson said. "Let's see it."

"Hey, suppose we just get out of here, okay?"

"Bring it over!"

Alma hesitated, then took the flare out of the compartment. She started toward Jackson. But before she could hand it to him, she realized her feet were moving out from under her.

"Help—I'm sinking," she cried out.

"What?"

Jackson felt the earth beneath his body begin to shift. He lifted his head out of the fissure, turned to see Alma, and realized the earth was opening up. They tried to throw themselves backward, but the ground fell away too fast. Alma screamed as she fell. They lost sight of each other tumbling as though in a long, curving drain—and then dropped down into blackness.

It seemed forever to Jackson before he landed on what felt like a steep slope of gravel. He slid farther, a rush of stones and ore washing downward with him. He choked from the dust and finally reached bottom—afraid to move.

Alma's screams had stopped.

Jackson called into the inky blackness. "Can you hear me?"

Alma's trembling voice came back at him. *"Jeez."*

"You okay?"

"I think so," she sputtered, unable to see him. "How about you?"

Jackson tested his arms and legs, stretching them. "I think I'm okay. No broken bones."

They lay silent, struggling to catch their breath. "Oh, God, I bet that thing is down here," Alma said.

Jackson decided not to think about that possibility. "No—it's an empty mine shaft." His hand felt a piece of stone the size of an arrowhead. He decided to put it in his pocket—to check it later if he ever got out alive.

"The ground's still moving," Alma said.

"Where's the flare?"

"I dropped it."

"You still have your camera?"

Alma felt down to the bulge in the side of her jeans. "Yes," she said, wiggling the camera out of her pocket.

Jackson said, "It's got a strobe flash, right?"

"If it's working."

"Try it."

Alma clutched the camera tightly, moving her fingers over it like reading Braille. She found the shutter button. "Here goes," she said.

The strobe flashed. Alma glimpsed what was causing the motion at her feet. A moving carpet of wedge-shaped heads with yellow eyes stared up at her from a churning mass of black, scaly coils.

"Snakes!" she screamed as the darkness crashed back in. She hit the button again and again, but it took a moment for the flash to recharge. When it finally fired, the blazing light startled the snakes further as they scrambled to escape.

"EEEEE!" Alma screamed again. She sucked in the dusty air. Her throat tightened as the head of one of the snakes snapped up at her face. She dropped the camera.

Jackson had watched for the flash. He saw Alma and the snakes several feet from him. The emergency flare was midway between them.

"They're probably harmless," Jackson shouted.

"PROBABLY?" Alma screamed back at him.

"Press the flash again."

He crawled along the floor of the cave, feeling in front of him for the flare.

"I dropped the camera."

"Get it."

"I can't."

"GET IT!"

Alma reached down into the darkness. Her hand touched a squirming, skinny body and fear grabbed her throat. At last she felt the small plastic rectangle. She lifted the camera, searching for the shutter button again. The flash fired. The last of the snakes were fleeing, but now there were several glistening, amorphous globs crawling up her arms. The darkness swallowed her and she dropped the camera again.

"They're slugs," Jackson shouted to her.

She flailed to rip them off her skin. She was sure she felt large unseen insects climbing up her neck and moving in her hair.

Jackson grasped the flare. "I'm coming." He scratched at its surface, but it wouldn't spark.

Alma's cries stopped.

"Are you all right?" he asked.

"Jackson . . ." Her voice came from the dark.

"What?"

"What are you chewing?"

"I'm not chewing. I'm trying to light the flare."

Alma was confused. His voice sounded a distance from her, but his breathing seemed to be right next to her. It came closer, and a pair of clammy lips touched the right side of her face.

She reached her hand up to his head. In the dark his hair felt coarser, longer than she had thought it would be. She felt a hand on her legs. "Are you touching me?"

"No," Jackson said.

The cap sparked and the tip of the flare burst into a white magnesium light. Jackson's pupils narrowed to shut out the small sun; then he looked beyond it.

Alma was frozen, staring at him from across the floor of the cave.

"Jackson . . ." Alma said.

"Don't move," he told her.

Small, pale faces and a collection of tiny limbs surrounded Alma in the pulsing light of the flare. The distended brow and albino face of a creature the size of a chimpanzee was smiling at her. Alma stared down. Other small, pale creatures with heads resembling those of bizarre human babies were stroking her legs and arms, picking slugs and insects from her body and eating them.

"Don't make a sound," Jackson said, crawling toward her with the flare.

ROAR

The horrifying sound reverberated from deep in the labyrinth of the cave. The sparkle faded quickly from the faces of the creatures surrounding Alma. They shrieked like terrified monkeys. Jackson got quickly to his feet and pulled Alma up. "We're out of here."

One of the smaller creatures with a fat, pink face grasped Alma's left leg.

ANOTHER ROAR. Closer now.

The creatures around them modulated their shrieks higher and higher into the shrill screams of a madhouse.

Alma saw her camera on the floor of the cave. She grabbed it, shoved it into her pocket. "I've heard of a dysfunctional family before," Alma wailed, "but this is ridiculous."

Jackson set the burning flare into the ground and pulled Alma away from the roaring.

"You're leaving the flare?"

"It'd make us look like spinner baits in a pike pond!"

Jackson ran with her to the far side of the cavern, where clusters of red stalactites framed the mine corridors. Suddenly, they were aware of the distant sound of a barking dog.

"Coffin!" Alma said.

"This way."

They began scrambling up a steep terraced wall of the main chamber. Soon they stumbled onto an incline of rotting railway ties and rusted mine track.

"Hurry," Jackson shouted.

Alma climbed fast in front of him. The slope of the tracks leveled off at a point several stories above the cavern floor. As Jackson and Alma crossed to the next incline, the roar of Skull Face exploded from below. Jackson grabbed Alma and made her stop. Breathing hard, she looked at him as if he were out of his mind.

SHHHHHHHH

They froze. Beyond the brink of the ledge, the roars of the beast rose toward them with the shrill cries of the smaller hominids. Carefully, Jackson and Alma peered over the edge. The beast was below, its great glistening skull head radiant, saliva dripping from its open, fanged jaws. It roared again, swiping at the smaller hominids, which scampered away from him shrieking in pain and protest. The full impact of the beast's rage was directed against the burning flare. It screamed at it as though it were a foreign god that had violated the lair.

Suddenly the roaring stopped. The smaller hominids quieted and crawled into the crannies along the edge of the cave floor. Alma turned away, fought to stop her knees from shaking. Jackson's gaze stayed riveted below. He saw the beast shifting gears, sniffing at the air in the way he had seen it do when its sickening face had been inches from the other side of the Plexiglas of the chopper window. The view from above made the creature's shoulders appear broader, more gnarled and deformed with muscle. It appeared to go into a trance, as though it were summoning up an instinct beyond smell or hearing.

TICK TICK

Jackson heard the ticking sounds. They seemed to come from a type of snapping back of the monster's tongue against the roof of its mouth. The creature scanned the cave with its mechanical sound. Slowly it lifted its head and stared up at Jackson. Its eyes locked onto his like lasers, and Jackson realized the ticking sounds of the monster were a homing device.

"Let's go," Alma cried. She scrambled up toward the sound of Coffin barking. Jackson started after her along the ledge, keeping his eyes fixed on the beast. The creature mimicked Jackson's speed and motion. It moved along the floor of the cave, circling toward the incline of the tracks and terracing.

"I see light," Alma called back to Jackson. She started to run up the steeply graded tracks.

Jackson saw the light, too, and the frame of the steel door at the end of the tunnel. He looked behind him, saw the creature had started up after them. Jackson resisted running, sensed it would trigger the creature's stalking pace into a full-speed attack. He wanted Alma to get as far ahead as possible—but terror made him pick up his pace. The beast accelerated with him.

Suddenly, Jackson lost control. He started to run. He glanced over his shoulder. The beast was bounding after them now. It was knuckle-running, loping like a gorilla in an all-out charge.

"Hurry," Alma screamed as she neared the top. At her shriek a great flapping of black, shiny wings exploded into life. She tripped on a piece of rotting track and reached out to the side of the shaft to break her fall. Her hand sank deep into a living fabric of bats.

"EEEEE!"

Jackson heard the thundering, cracking sounds of the beast fast behind him. He saw Alma make it out beyond the steel door, and glimpsed the red of the dune buggy and Coffin straining against his leash.

"It's going to get you!" Alma screamed. She

skirted the hole through which they'd fallen and leaped up out of the hollow.

Jackson reached the door. He swung it behind him with all his might.

CLANG

"It won't close!" he cried out.

Alma saw him struggling. "There's a stone blocking it."

The monster planted its fists and arms like crutches, lurching forward with ferocious swings. Jackson kicked at the stone.

It wouldn't budge.

In a second Alma was back at his side. Together they pushed until the stone rolled clear.

They slammed the door shut as the beast crashed into it. Alma threw a locking bolt into place, as the beast pounded savagely, a series of booming, deafening blows that caused the entire door frame to shudder.

Without looking back, Jackson and Alma raced up out of the hollow. Jackson started the buggy. Alma threw Coffin's leash off the bumper.

"Come on!" Jackson yelled.

Alma leaped up to straddle the backseat. He threw the shift into gear and opened the throttle wide. The buggy shot out from the mouth of the hollow, propelling them away from the sounds of Hell.

~8~

TRILITHONS

Jackson drove full tilt, with Coffin racing off to the left of the buggy like a dolphin pacing a boat to harbor. Alma scanned the ground beneath them, no longer trusting it.

"That was horrible," Alma said, her arms locked tightly around Jackson's waist. "We've got to tell Tillman and Rath."

"No way. The army'll flood the cave or blow it up. They'd slaughter *all* the hominids, not just Skull Face. He's the supermutant. Those little guys picking bugs off you weren't killers."

"Stop talking about those things like they're human!"

"They *are*! Well, almost."

Jackson doubled back several hundred yards along a dirt road and made it into the Stonehenge parking lot. Even Coffin seemed to know there was safety in numbers as packs of tourists flowed in and out of the entrance gates and souvenir shop. Jackson pulled the buggy to a halt between a parked tour bus and a minivan.

He remembered the piece of stone he'd found that was shaped like an arrowhead, and took it out of his pocket. It was black and shiny in the sunlight. "It's flint, right?"

"Of course it is."

"We have to call my aunt," Jackson said, slipping the piece of flint back into his pants pocket.

"There are no pay phones here," Alma said, sliding down off the backseat. She started brushing off the dirt that had accumulated on her clothing in the fall into the cave. "My stomach's doing flips—I need tea. You got any money?"

Jackson got off the buggy and checked deeper in his pockets. He found a five-pound note and a handful of change.

"Two teas and two scones," Alma ordered. "And get something for yourself."

"You're having *two* teas?"

"One's for Coffin," Alma said. "He takes five creamers."

Jackson dusted himself off as he walked across the lot to the snack stand. By the time he got back, Alma and Coffin were collapsed on the grass near a picnic table.

"Why are all those terrible things growing down there?" Alma took one of the steaming Styrofoam cups of tea and set it in front of Coffin.

"I don't know," Jackson said.

Coffin's eyes widened watching Alma toss creamer after creamer into his tea. Next she buttered a scone. He grabbed it and chewed it on the grass.

Alma groaned. "It's like Nature's gone berserk down in that cave."

"Maybe it's the chemicals from the biochem factory," Jackson said. "My aunt told me about a mangrove swamp where nature has no rules. The fish climb trees. The roots of the trees grow upward. That swamp is a hundred square miles of killers—tigers who eat people. The tigers have nothing to drink but salt water with strange chemicals, and it affects their brains."

"I think I've heard enough."

"No," Jackson said. "The tigers are like Skull Face. They stalk and are rarely seen. They understand humans and never attack when a human is facing them. Natives started wearing face masks on the backs of their heads when they walked through the swamp. The tigers caught on. They could tell the real faces from the masks."

"That's horrible."

"The natives don't think so. They think the tigers

are gods. They believe the tigers were sent from heaven to protect their swamp and forest. They stop the land from being exploited. Those tigers are not a legend, Alma. They're scientific fact. So is what's growing under the ground around here. Don't you realize what we've found? What's down in that cave is older than anything we can imagine. It was kids who found one of the most important caves in France that was filled with prehistoric art. It made them famous."

Alma stood up, wadded her napkin, and hurled it into a trash container. "Well, that's just swell—except that *our* prehistoric art wants to eat us."

"Only Skull Face. The little guys are cool. They were smiling, partying as they took the slugs and bugs off you. Alma, we were in the presence of an entirely different species of hominids. They weren't at all like the super-mutant monster. They looked like our friendly little cousins, didn't they?"

"Not my cousins." Alma saw the excitement in Jackson's face. "All I know is somebody's got to stop Skull Face before it kills again."

She looked past the entrance gates and across to Stonehenge. The monument stood fabulous, mysterious in the blazing sun. Jackson got up and stood next to her.

"First we tell my aunt," he said.

~

Dr. Cawley was in her room at the hospital when Jackson phoned. He had dropped Alma off at the High Street Gate of Salisbury Close and driven back to Langford's to make the call.

At first Jackson talked so fast his aunt could barely understand him. "They're pale and weird, like a tribe of midget Cro-Magnons." His voice exploded from Dr. Cawley's receiver. "They're little versions of the big guy, but without the fangs. And they're friendly. They picked snails and bugs off Alma, and . . ."

Dr. Cawley stopped him in mid sentence. She knew her phone could be tapped. "I'll call Tillman. He'll arrange for a car to bring you here. Are you sure Alma can keep her mouth shut?"

"Alma's terrific."

Dr. Cawley hung up as the head nurse on the afternoon shift came in with tiny, squeaky steps. She wore a stiff, white nurse's cap and carried a clipboard.

"I'm Sister Thornton-Sherwood." She glanced at the chart hanging from the bottom of Dr. Cawley's bed. "You must be exhausted from your tests this morning. You had a problem during the CAT scan?"

Without waiting for a response, she started checking the linen and bedstand supplies of the vacant bed.

Dr. Cawley asked, "What are you doing?"

Sister Thornton-Sherwood jotted on her notepad as she talked. "You're getting a roommate."

"Dr. Halperin said I was to have a private room."

"Well, he forgot to tell us. Our rooms are double occupancy. They're bringing her up from Admitting. A mature woman."

Dr. Cawley forced a smile. She wanted the nurse to know she'd be accommodating. She had shared sleeping rooms with a wide slice of humanity, from a voodoo priestess in Haiti to a half dozen Japanese men in a climbing shack on Mount Fuji.

An attendant came in pushing an oxygen tank on a dolly.

"Set it up there," the nurse ordered, indicating a spot next to the empty bed.

The smile faded from Dr. Cawley's face. She didn't mean to speak, but a voice was forming in her brain. She fought against the voice, but she found a single word slipping out of her throat. "No."

Sister Thornton-Sherwood looked up from her clipboard. She was surprised, but immune to patients trying to run things. "Did you say something?"

Dr. Cawley tried to remain silent. The voice in her brain was clear, controlling her vocal cords and her thoughts. "The room next door is empty," she said. Her hands began to shake. "Why don't you put the patient in there?"

"Because I decided she will be in *here*."

"No oxygen tank. No patient" were the words that came from Dr. Cawley's lips. She locked eyes with Sister Thornton-Sherwood as the attendant halted setting up the tank. "I don't want anyone else in this room."

"Look," Sister Thornton-Sherwood said, "I told you this is a double room and—"

"GET OUT!" Dr. Cawley suddenly shouted. The force was inside her; it stretched her vocal cords, made her scream like an animal. "THIS IS MY ROOM! MINE! BOTH OF YOU GET OUT!"

Sister Thornton-Sherwood looked as if a thorn had been pressed into her heart. She considered the situation, then motioned the attendant to roll the tank out of the room. She checked Dr. Cawley's chart again. "Apparently you have a problem with claustrophobia," she said, in a low voice.

Dr. Cawley felt her face flush, her eyes narrow with rage. She was certain it was connected to Ramid's bite.

"Yes," Dr. Cawley said, struggling to calm herself. "I *do* have claustrophobia."

Sister Thornton-Sherwood watched Dr. Cawley deflate, sink back into the pillows of her bed.

"Perhaps while you're here," Sister Thornton-Sherwood said, "Dr. Halperin will insist you see a psychiatrist."

~

"How are things out at the cemetery?" Jackson pumped the young soldier for news as they zipped along the A36 in a landrover. Tillman had sent a newly promoted man, Sergeant Keyes, to drive Jackson to the hospital.

"It's round-the-clock duty," the soldier said. "There's few of us left out there. The rest of the search company was moved south this afternoon."

Sergeant Keyes was in his late twenties, his hair cut into a designer crew look. He had a small scar to the left of his lower lip. "Lieutenant Rath had the men looking north, but a recon team turned up a mess of tracks and activity near Amesbury."

Jackson understood it meant the search for Skull Face was closing in on Stonehenge.

The soldier waited until he had the landrover off the highway and onto the Bristol streets before he got personal. "Sorry your aunt's having problems."

Jackson noticed there was a wariness in Keyes' voice. "What are you talking about?"

"Hey, I figured you knew about it."

"About what?"

"I heard the call to Tillman when it came in. Something about your aunt drawing on walls. The hospital called to tell Tillman the army would have to pay for the damage." Keyes pulled the landrover up to the main entrance of the hospital and stopped. Jackson jumped out and dashed for the front door.

"I'll be waiting in the coffee shop," Sergeant Keyes called after him.

Jackson grabbed a visitor's pass from the reception desk and took the elevator to the ninth floor. He got off, walked quickly down the corridor following the arrows to the South Wing. Sister Thornton-Sherwood with her clipboard intercepted him as he passed the nurses' station. "Are you Dr. Cawley's nephew?"

Jackson looked at the nurse's ticked-off face. "What's going on?"

The nurse clicked her ballpoint. "Does your aunt have any history of mental illness? Is she on an anti-depressant?"

Jackson spun on his heels, broke into a jog down the hall.

"It's not my fault," the nurse called after him. "She asked us for blank paper. I told her she'd have to wait for the gift-shop cart like everybody else."

The door to his aunt's room was closed. Jackson

knocked on the door hard, opened it, and went in.

Dr. Cawley stood in her bathrobe in front of the long high-gloss white wall across from her bed. Her back was to Jackson as her right hand lashed out with bold strokes of a felt-tipped pen—the final details of a turbulent mural. It was a sketch of Stonehenge as it must have looked when its stones were all complete and upright.

Jackson closed the door behind him. "Aunt Sarah, are you okay?"

"Right this minute, yes," Dr. Cawley said without turning around. "In another minute maybe not."

She threw the pen to the floor and grabbed a large black Magic Marker. Her last strokes on the mural were to the largest of the sarsen stones in the middle of the circle.

"Aunt Sarah . . ."

Finally she turned to him. "Jackson, I think I'm losing my mind—but in a very thrilling way," she said oddly, brushing her fingers repeatedly through her hair. She smiled, went to him, and gave him a big hug.

"Sit," she told him, indicating a brown plastic-covered armchair.

"I know I'm frightening you," she said, "but I've got to talk while I can. Something's happening to me." She sat on her bed.

"What, Aunt Sarah?"

"It's from the monster's bite. Not rabies. It's like what you get in Europe from the bite of a street animal. A delirium. It's like that. As if Ramid—that's what I've decided to call the creature—has passed some crawling thing into my blood."

"Aunt Sarah, should I get the doctor?"

"No. I've got to tell you this quickly, because sometimes my mind quits on me," Dr. Cawley said. "The problem is that I feel too good, and no doctor around here is going to treat me for that. When my mind's functioning, it's razor sharp. It's like Ramid's blood or saliva was composed of computer chips. Smart blood. I get to glimpse things I didn't know on my own.

"When I came back from my tests, I was lying in bed. I could feel the spirit of Ramid hovering over me like a spirit that had control over my brain. I know this sounds quite mad, but I began to wonder if maybe this new species has evolved its own intelligence. A biomechanical brilliance that allows the monster to control its cells and fluids over great distances. I don't know."

Jackson looked past his aunt to the huge drawing on the wall behind her.

"Aunt Sarah, why did you draw Stonehenge?"

"I drew it because . . ."

Jackson watched as the manic brightness of her eyes faded. She opened her mouth as an agony twisted and stole its way into her body. "Ramid is trying to stop me from thinking about it," she gasped. "From thinking about the trilithons."

Jackson stood up. "I'll get help . . ."

Dr. Cawley motioned him to be still. She grabbed a lipstick from her pocketbook and rushed to the mural. "Here . . ." she said, fighting to force the words out before Ramid had complete control again. "Don't forget . . . *here!*"

She managed to rub the lipstick onto one of the horizontal stones, the top of an archway inside the circle. Trembling, she put her hands into the shiny redness and dragged the color with her fingertips high up the wall. The crimson streaked as though the one stone were setting the sky on fire.

Jackson turned her from the painting.

"You should lie down, Aunt Sarah . . ."

"DOOM!" she started to shout, as she wrote the word above the stone. "The trilithons with the Stone of Doom!"

She was shaking, stripped of her voice again as he got her back onto the bed. Her two-way radio was on the bedstand. Jackson looked for the room's emergency buzzer. When he couldn't find it, he ran out into the hall. "Get a doctor!" he shouted, running toward the nurses' station.

Sister Thornton-Sherwood came fast from another patient's room. "What's wrong?"

"Just help her!"

"Page Dr. Nielsen," Sister Thornton-Sherwood shot to a nurses' aide behind the desk.

He saw the expression on Sister Thornton-Sherwood's face suddenly change from irritation to surprise. He realized she was looking behind him and turned. Dr. Cawley was strolling down the hall toward them and strangely smiling.

"Aunt Sarah?" Jackson said, puzzled.

Sister Thornton-Sherwood put her hand in her pocket to check for a hypodermic she had readied. "You should rest in your room, Dr. Cawley."

"I would like some beef," Dr. Cawley said.

Sister Thornton-Sherwood rolled her eyes. "We're very sorry, Dr. Cawley," she said, as if she were talking to an infantile madwoman, "but today is Friday and that means chicken or fish. Our chef doesn't cook beef on Fridays."

Dr. Cawley said, "I smell beef."

The nurse put her arm around Dr. Cawley and started to turn her back toward her room. "Now,

now . . . the kitchen is nine floors down. Even if we had beef, which we *don't*, you couldn't smell it up here."

"I SMELL BEEF!" Dr. Cawley screamed, pounding her fist on the counter of the nurses' station. *"BEEF!"*

Sister Thornton-Sherwood let go of Dr. Cawley and grabbed the P.A. mike. "Dr. Nielsen to S9 Station! Dr. Nielsen, S9 emergency!"

Two hulking attendants appeared at the end of the hall and ran toward them. Dr. Cawley turned suddenly, desperately, to Jackson. "Don't tell where the hominids are," she said, starting to wheeze and choke. "Don't tell anyone until I get out of here. And the trilithons! Don't forget the trilithons! Doom! Doom! *Promise me!"*

"I promise," Jackson said quickly. "I promise."

"BEEF!" Dr. Cawley found herself screaming again. "BEEF! GIVE ME BEEF!"

~9~
WAITING

Alma knew Salisbury Cathedral and the red-brick buildings of the close as well as she knew the back of her hand. The vast cathedral with its huge tower and spire had been under repair for years—since the time when her father was one of the close gardeners. Steel pipe and rough-hewed plank walkways still covered vast sections of the cathedral's leaded roof. Scaffolding in the shape of octagonal platforms circled its spire up to the pinnacle like a trio of rings on a ringtoss.

Alma smiled as she crossed the main green and saw familiar faces. Many evenings, when the McPhees had lived at the close, Alma had baby-sat for the children of the masons and construction crews.

"Hi, Reverend!" she called across to the black-frocked Reverend Kalley on Bishop's Walk.

The cleric waved when he recognized her. "Welcome back, Alma."

"Do you know where they put us?" she asked. She

knew the Reverend Kalley usually knew everything that was happening at the close.

"In the Canonry, I think. The basement flat." He smiled, pleased that he could help.

Alma felt warm and safe back inside the close grounds. The smell of arbored wisteria and fresh-mowed spring grass made the horror of Skull Face and the creepy little hominids seem far away. She wished they could live at the close permanently. She had often daydreamed about just that, had visions of being able to walk to school and to live in a place where friends weren't spooked if they stopped by. Of course, part of the dream was that her mother would come back and they could be a real family again.

By sunset the kitchen boxes were unpacked at the apartment. Alma had fed Coffin and defrosted a shepherd's pie and lemon cake for her and her father's dinner. "We can finish the rest of the boxes tomorrow," her dad said, putting on his favorite sweater and baggy brown polyester pants. "I'm taking a stroll to pick up some smokes."

"Okay, Dad," Alma said. "Be careful, okay?"

"Yes, darlin'."

Alma knew "picking up smokes" really meant he was going out to the pubs, which was what her mom had hated most about him—his drinking and late hours. He'd start at the Haunch of Venison Inn, then ale and bitter his way past Poultry Cross and all the way to Queen Street. As soon as he was out the door, Alma threw off her clothes and jumped into the shower. She was drying herself with a faded blue towel when Jackson phoned.

"Did you have trouble getting through?" Alma asked.

"A little," Jackson said. "First they connected me to the bishop's palace, then the cloister operator. She knew where to ring."

"Where are you?"

"I'm still in Bristol—in the hospital lobby. I'll be back by nine. It's a little crazy here," Jackson said.

Alma heard the strain in his voice. "What's the matter?"

"Aunt Sarah's hallucinating. She's treating her room like it's her territory and she's an animal."

"An animal?"

"I was with her when she could smell roast beef cooking nine floors below and it wasn't on the menu. Her wires are crossed—it's got to be from Skull Face's bite. She's calm one minute, then freaks out and yells. She's been drawing Stonehenge on her walls. She rubbed lipstick onto one of the top stones and shouted, 'Doom! The trilithons with the Stone of Doom!' "

"The trilithons? A Stone of Doom?"

"She kept saying DOOM! DOOM! DOOM!"

"Trilithons are those biggest stones inside the circle."

"I know—arranged like a big horseshoe. The doctors say she has a fever, but they won't know how to treat her unless they can run tests on the animal that bit her."

"We've got to tell the army where Skull Face's lair is," Alma said. "We've got to."

"Aunt Sarah said we shouldn't tell anybody anything until she gets back. Maybe she's afraid Rath'll just order troops in with flamethrowers. Maybe the little guys'll rewrite every evolution theory in the book. Maybe they're the cure for cancer. Who knows?"

"We've got to do something!" Alma's voice broke. "We can't just sit around and let Skull Face kill anybody else!"

"Do you still have your camera?"

Alma stumbled across to where she'd dropped her clothes. She dug through the pockets of her jeans until she saw the camera's thin slab of black plastic. "I've got it."

"We have to develop the film. When you were using the flash, you might have gotten a shot of the hominids. We have to check it out A.S.A.P."

"There's no photo shops open at this hour."

"I know how to develop. Is there a darkroom at the close?"

"No." Alma's mind raced through all the kids she knew who were into photography. She felt a chill start on her legs, then crawl fast up her spine. "The only darkroom I know is out at the crematorium. The undertakers make extra money with it. Families want videos and photos of the memorial services. Some want shots of their loved ones in their caskets."

"Can you get us in there?"

"When?"

"Tonight."

"Are you crazy?"

Jackson thought a moment. "Probably," he finally said. "Try to check out those books in the cathedral library. The ones with the freakiest theories about Stonehenge. See if there's anything about a Trilithon Stone of Doom. Then meet me at Langford's garage at ten."

~

Sergeant Keyes got Jackson back to Langford's a half hour before Alma was to meet him. He went directly upstairs to the apartment.

His aunt's research books and sketches were still strewn about the sitting room like jagged pieces of a frightening puzzle. He got the large, worn-leather book on Stonehenge and pulled a chair up to the oak table. The clay cast of the jaws of the beast loomed over him like the draped head of a cadaver.

He skimmed through the book looking for engravings of the trilithons. Several drawings showed them as five sets of massive stones that had originally stood in the shape of a horseshoe around an altar, but he couldn't find anything about what they were used for. He took the book downstairs with him to wait for Alma.

"A trip to the moon . . . wings . . ."

The piano player was singing for the late dinner crowd as Jackson slipped quietly down the staircase and out the door. He saw Mrs. Langford through a vast slab of windows as he headed down the driveway. She was seating a group of guests at a table in the dining room. The chef and kitchen workers were too busy to notice him go by.

He made his way without a flashlight past the carports and herb garden. In the garage, he pulled the string of the single overhead light. The naked bulb blazed, then swung in the night breeze, causing shadows to crawl across the floor.

Jackson set the book down on the dune buggy seat and began rummaging through the army surplus equipment. The thing he spotted right off was a two-way radio. He flicked the power switch and an indicator lit up. He tossed the radio into the storage compartment of the buggy.

There were crunching sounds on the gravel driveway. A figure came toward him into the light spilling from the garage. It was Alma, her long thick hair pulled back into a ponytail. The expression on her face was dead serious.

"I'm glad it's you," Jackson said. He took the book from the seat and handed it to her.

"What's this?"

"One of my aunt's books. It might have something about trilithons."

"I checked through the oldest book in the cathedral library," Alma said. "It's huge. The pages are handwritten on big parchment pages. It has a whole section about a monster that's supposed to have stalked the land around here for centuries. It sounds like Skull Face."

"Anything about a Doom Stone?"

"A lot written in Latin and Old English. From what I could make out, there was a stone that had been found at Stonehenge. It had an inscription on it:

> "'And no stone
>   Where there was stone,
>   In the Tomb
>   Of the final Doom.'"

"It sounds like a riddle," Jackson said.

"Half the book is written in riddles—as if whoever wrote it was afraid to just come right out and talk about the monster."

"Or *think* about it." Jackson reached down into a trunk and pulled out a fat-barreled pistol.

Alma frowned. "No guns. I hate guns."

"This one's okay," Jackson said, loading a large shotgun-type cartridge into its double chamber. "It's a flare gun. If we fall down any more flint mines, we can fire a flare."

He opened the compartment under the rear seat of the buggy and dropped the loaded flare gun into it next to the radio—along with a couple of extra flare cartridges. His eye caught a strange set of electronic-looking goggles hanging from a nail toward the back of the garage. He grabbed them.

Alma shook her head. "We don't need a gas mask."

"Wrong," Jackson said, slipping the goggles on. He reached up and yanked the string on the bulb.

"Hey, I can't see," Alma complained in the dark.

Jackson clicked on a switch at the side of the goggles. Instantly, Alma and the inside of the garage became a pulsing green and shimmering landscape. He reached out and clamped his hand on Alma's shoulder. She jumped a foot. "What are you doing?"

Jackson put the garage light back on. "These are night-vision goggles. Probably one of the first models the army ever made." He tossed the goggles into the compartment with the flare gun and radio.

"Let's take your aunt's book, too," Alma said.

"Right," Jackson said. "No point in leaving any stone unturned."

~10~
FIRE

Jackson gassed the dune buggy up the slope past the Old Sarum ruins to a fork in the path.

"Turn left," Alma said. "We'll make good time going up through Woodford. There are no Ministry of Defense lands or training grounds, and the farmers don't get too disturbed about strangers on their dirt roads."

A fog rose from the Avon and brooked across the valley toward them. Dark rolling clouds drifted low like the hulls of sailing ships to blot out the stars. Farther on the headlights of the buggy picked up a field of scrub evergreens, and sheep lay like ghosts among the grass barrows.

"Just keep us away from Skull Face territory," Jackson said. "The buggy's faster than him, but I'd rather not put it to the test. Where's Coffin?"

"In my room at the close. I left him food and water," Alma added. "He'd bark like crazy in Woodford. It's famous for witches."

"Nice. Did you find out what the trilithons were used for?"

"Nobody knows exactly."

"You're telling me that a bunch of people thousands of years ago decided to lug a mess of forty-five-ton stones over twenty miles—that's after they already carried a load of the blue stones two hundred miles from Wales . . ."

"They probably floated the blue stones part of the way on rafts."

"These folks went to all the mind-boggling pain and exhaustion of setting up the biggest stones into a horseshoe *and nobody knows why*?"

"What's your point?"

"Wouldn't you think they built the trilithons for an important reason? Ten uprights. Five humongous stones laid on top of those. Can you imagine these humans sitting around a campfire one night and saying, 'Hey, wouldn't it be fun to bust our chops for a dozen decades or more and lug some *really* massive stones down here to make a horseshoe that doesn't mean anything?' "

"What are you getting at?"

"Does the word 'sacrifice' mean anything to you?" Jackson asked. "A huge horseshoe with an altar stone smack in the middle of it looks and sounds like a great place to knock off people—or *something*."

The headlights from the buggy hit an eroding hillside, making thick veins of exposed chalk look like ice melting from swollen black teeth.

"What trilithon did your aunt put the lipstick on?" Alma asked.

"The one in the middle of the horseshoe—the top stone."

Alma pictured the stones in her mind. "That stone's missing. A lot of the stones at Stonehenge have fallen over or are missing. Many of them were taken, cut up, and used to build farmhouses and churches. Some could have been used in Salisbury Cathedral. I thought that might be what was meant by the first two lines of the old inscription—*And no stone Where there was stone. . . .*"

"Could be," Jackson agreed, "but what does *In the Tomb Of the final Doom* mean?"

"I don't know."

Farther north the fog spilled thicker from the river, vertical wisps gliding at them like spectral, ashen sailors. Quickly, the visibility dropped dangerously. Jackson switched on the buggy's fog lights, and the mist became a wall of blood. A flock of night crows chattered like teeth, then screamed and flew up to feast on a hive of bees in the hollow of a dead oak.

Jackson was grateful for the cover of the fog as they approached the cemetery. He had switched off the headlights, kept only the red fogs.

"The crematorium's a couple of hundred feet ahead," Alma said.

Jackson shut the lights and switched off the engine. He helped Alma down from the buggy. She flipped up the rear seat and took the thick leather book out of the compartment. Jackson grabbed the night-vision goggles. "You'll need these," he said, helping her set them into place over her eyes. He clicked the battery switch on. She signaled she could see as voices of soldiers drifted at them through the fog from the encampment on the edge of the plain.

"They're playing cards," Jackson figured out from their voices. A moment later, he thought he heard Sergeant Keyes' laughter. Slowly, Alma led the way.

~

Mr. McPhee had two ales and bitters before he returned to the close. He'd chatted with a crony at the Black Swan Inn and was tempted to tie on a good one—but he thought of Alma. He had felt a sense of pride about being allowed to stay back at the close while the army searched for the cockamamie monster. He was reminded of the good life he'd had there. The clergy had treated him respectfully. He'd long felt guilty about making Alma move to the cemetery, but she'd never thrown it up in his face. For that he loved her dearly.

As he opened the door to the Canonry apartment, he thought kindly of his wife. "You'd come back if we lived here, you would," he muttered aloud, as though she were in the hallway with him. "I'd try hard not to burn the bottoms out of pots or stink up the place with cigars. I'd do more with the cleanin', and take you and Alma out to sing karaoke . . ."

The apartment was dusty from the unpacking. He left the front door open to let in the fresh night air. He flicked on the hall light and hung his cardigan up in the closet.

"Alma?" he called. "Alma?"

He heard Coffin start to bark—then saw the note on the kitchen table: *Dad, I've gone out with Jackson. See you later. Love, Alma.*

Mr. McPhee smiled. He was glad she was with the American boy. He knew the local boys made fun of her because she had a gravedigger for a father. But it couldn't be helped.

Coffin scratched at the floor inside Alma's room. "Okay, okay, don't go diggin' to China," Mr. McPhee said. He was used to Coffin kicking up a fuss whenever Alma went out and left him behind. He stood to one side. Coffin would, as always, bound out and crash into him, then whip him painfully with his tail. After that, without fail, the dog would leap up, slap his front paws down hard on Mr. McPhee's shoulders, and start licking his face.

"Here I am, boy," Mr. McPhee said, opening the door and braced for the eruption.

The massive blur of shaggy fur flew out of the room. Mr. McPhee put out his hand to brace himself, but Coffin ran smack past him.

"Hey!" Mr. McPhee called out. The dog raced for the hall, his huge paws skidding as he turned on the waxed wide-planked floors. Before Mr. McPhee could stop him, Coffin was out the front door.

Mr. McPhee rushed after him, shouting, "Come back, you lout!" He watched the dog fly across the close like a race horse.

"Coffin! Coffin!" Mr. McPhee shouted as he ran on for a distance across the grass. He noticed a group of frocked men moving out from the shadows of the towering cathedral and knew he shouldn't shout or they'd think he was drunk. He stopped, gasping for air, and watched as Coffin disappeared through the North Gate.

~

Alma opened the combination lock on the heavy steel cellar doors of the crematorium. They were flush with the ground and lifted like a pair of flaps on a box to reveal a set of damp cement steps.

"No lights or the soldiers will come snooping," Jackson said.

"What if they think *we're* the monster?" Alma asked.

"They won't."

"But they *could*. We might look like the beast in the fog. They might have set a trap. Or they could shoot us—did you think about that?"

"They won't know we're here," Jackson said, feeling his way to close the cellar doors behind them.

Alma adjusted her night-vision goggles, reached out to take his hand, and led him down into the main cremation room.

"You wanted to see what the furnace looks like," Alma said, taking off the goggles and handing them to him. Jackson slipped them on and saw the room bathed in a bright, ghastly green. It was a half cellar with a row of narrow windows lining the top of weeping cinder-block walls. In the middle of the room lay the cremation furnace.

"It *does* look like a Chirping Chicken grill," Jackson had to admit.

"There's another, more modern furnace upstairs. It's in a viewing room that's like a stage. It's for cremation services where the relatives want to see their loved one cranked into the flames."

Jackson reached out to touch the safety cage over the furnace. It resembled a zoo cage complete with a door. "Where's the darkroom?"

He took the night-vision goggles off. Alma slipped them on and led him toward the rear wall. "In here," she said, opening a door and leading him into a small, narrow room.

"Put on the developing light," Jackson asked.

She threw a wall switch and a single red bulb cast a glow over the small room.

"Great."

Alma took the goggles off as Jackson closed the door and began checking out the equipment. There was a sink, a counter with shallow trays, and shelves with a half dozen gallon jugs of developing chemicals.

"Where's our film?" Jackson said.

Alma wiggled the camera out of her pocket and handed it to him. He pressed the automatic rewind, let it whirl to a stop, and flicked open the back of the camera. Jackson removed the cartridge and shut off the red light long enough for him to get the film itself into a circular black plastic canister. He began mixing fresh solutions from the chemicals.

CLANK

A sound from the furnace room.

"What's that?" Alma asked.

"The wind rattling the cellar doors," Jackson guessed.

Alma pulled up a stool under the glowing red bulb and started scanning the pages of the big book for anything remotely connected to the trilithons.

"The altar stone is presently half-buried in front of one of the trilithons," she said. "But it used to be a big slab lying right out on the ground."

Alma speed-read down the narrow type of the pages. "There's another stone they call the Slaughter Stone that has stains that look like blood from sacrifices. It says the stains are really from rains leaching out the iron content of the stone."

"What about the moon? It can't be an accident that it's almost a full moon and this monster is starting to kill." Jackson used a funnel to pour a solution into the developing canister and set the wall timer. "And if it *is* the moon, why doesn't the creature kill every twenty-seven days or something?"

"The guides tell everyone at Stonehenge how the moon is on a nineteen-year cycle," Alma said. "That the moon doesn't rise in the same positions every year like the sun does. It has a wobbly, elliptical orbit. It repeats its exact path only every nineteen years."

TICK

Alma heard the sound and stopped breathing.

TICK TICK

"I hear ticking," Alma said. She looked at a big-faced timer on the wall. "It's the timer."

"The timer's electric," Jackson said. "It doesn't tick."

TICK TICK TICK

Alma felt fingers of ice crawl around her heart.

TICK

The sound came from the wall behind them.

"Probably a steam pipe behind the wall," Jackson said.

"There's no wall or pipes there," Alma said. "This is a half cellar—there's just the cinder block and a small window. They covered it with plywood to make the darkroom."

The timer sounded. Jackson unscrewed the circular canister.

"What are you doing?" Alma said.

"The film has to be washed with water and fixed or it'll overdevelop."

"You're making *noise*."

"I have to."

"Skull Face is outside. Maybe he can see the red light. It could be leaking through the cracks of the top window. Or it could be the soldiers with guns."

TICK TICK TICK

The sounds were loud and clear now, like a Geiger counter hitting a vein of uranium. Alma put out the light.

"Hey, I can't see," Jackson said. He clutched the strip of negatives. Skull Face or no Skull Face, he had to rinse the chemicals off. He reached out in the dark, found the cold handle of the sink's faucet, and turned it on. He felt the cold rush of water hit the strip of negatives and hoped it would be enough to save the pictures. "Give me the goggles."

"I won't be able to see."

"I need them."

She held his arm as she took off the goggles. As he put them on, the ticking sounds from behind the wall came faster, louder. Seen through the night-vision goggles, everything in the darkroom was an eerie green. He held the film against the porcelain of the sink, saw the negatives of the shots Alma had taken of the soldiers canvassing the cemetery. Next on the strip was the shot of him and the dune buggy.

"We got something," he said. "It still needs a fixing bath."

"Shhhhhhh."

Something was captured in the flash shots of the cave. Negative images of snakes, and stones—and the smiling faces of little hominids.

CRASH

The sounds of breaking glass broke the silence of the darkroom. A split second later the plywood wall itself shattered, and a monstrous, gnarled arm flew in at them. The claws of the huge hand swept in a wide arc, straining to hook into its prey.

Alma screamed in the darkness. She knew from the sounds what was happening, felt Jackson grab her hand and pull her toward the door of the darkroom. In a moment he had the door unlocked and open, and was traveling fast toward the cellar doors.

Jackson looked over his shoulder, saw the creature bursting into the darkroom like a leviathan being born from an immense exploding egg.

Jackson hit his shoulder against the cellar doors. They wouldn't budge. Alma understood what he was doing, and pushed with him. Instantly she understood something chilling. "It's locked the doors!" she screamed. *"Skull Face locked us in!"*

"Stop screaming."

"It's smarter than us!"

"No, it isn't."

"It's going to get us!"

She reached out desperately for Jackson. He put his arm around her, pulled her back into the cremation room.

TICK TICK

Jackson faded left with Alma, putting the cage of the furnace between them and the monstrosity as it emerged from the destroyed darkroom.

"What's happening?" Alma screamed.

Jackson couldn't speak. The creature moved slowly toward them. Alma reached out, felt the metal of the furnace cage as they and the monstrosity circled it. Jackson kept one eye on Skull Face, another searching for a weapon—anything. "How do they get the ashes out of the furnace?" he asked Alma.

"There's a gate," she said. She realized what he was thinking. "You can open it."

"Where is it?"

"Facing the far wall."

The creature kept to Jackson's pace, its burning eyes staring out from the shadowed sockets of its skull. Its head was tilted and alert. Jackson knew its brain was on full reconnoiter, with dark, glistening fluids leaking from the crater that was its nose. Its twisted fangs stretched its lips wide.

"Can you see the gate?" Alma asked.

Jackson glanced left for a split second. The creature's head twitched as it picked up on Jackson scanning the obstacle between them.

"How does it open?" Jackson asked quickly.

"It opens in—there's no lock."

A shovel leaned against the furnace cage. Jackson waited until he was in position.

TICK TICK

"Go!" Jackson yelled, pushing Alma in through the gate. He pressed her head low, guiding it under the gas jets. Skull Face roared at the sudden move, came hurtling down the length of the cage. Jackson grabbed the shovel and dove inside after Alma. He jammed the latch with the shovel, and the latch held.

The goggles had slipped from Jackson's eyes, and he worked fast to set them straight. He saw that he and Alma were lying in a long metal tray beneath the gas jets.

"Are we safe?" Alma asked.

Jackson pulled her toward him, centering them both where the creature's claws couldn't reach them. "We're safe." He saw the specks on their clothes. "Is this tray used for what I think it's used for?"

Alma flattened her hand beneath her and felt the cold metal. "Yes."

Jackson felt nauseous.

All sounds stopped.

"What's going on?" Alma asked from her darkness.

Jackson surveyed the perimeter of the cage. "I can't see the creature."

TICK

The sound was above them now. An odor like rotting flesh wafted down, and Jackson laid his head back against the cold trough. He focused past the bed of gas jets. Skull Face was looking at him. The monster lay still on top of the furnace cage, staring intently, mucus from its nose dripping down upon Jackson's neck. From within the deathly glare of the monster's eyes small black pupils glared with a gruesome cunning.

"Skull Face is on top of the cage," Jackson said.

"What's he doing?"

"I think he's *memorizing* us."

The monstrosity turned to glare at Alma. Jackson was thankful she couldn't see. Drippings from the creature hit her arm, and she rubbed at the liquid, thinking it was condensation from the metal cage. The membrane covering Skull Face's head sparkled like a ghastly veil, a horrid, transparent mask binding the huge skull.

"Where are the soldiers?" Alma asked. "They must have heard the noise—heard me screaming."

"They could have thought the sounds came from the mill," Jackson said. "They'll come—don't worry."

TICK TICK

The hands of the creature crept like spiders along the sides of the cage. Its claws dug around the welded joints, seeking out any weak spots.

"How do you turn on the gas jets?" Jackson asked.

"Why?"

"Just tell me."

"There's a floor valve outside the gate."

Jackson turned onto his side. He could see the valve, with its flat chrome handle.

"What lights the gas?"

"A pilot light. It's automatic. Oh, God, you're going to cook us, aren't you?" said Alma.

As Jackson reached out toward the valve, Skull Face returned its stare to him. Its fetid breath burned in Jackson's nostrils as the reach of his arm and fingertips fell short of the valve handle. He saw a thin, metal rod, like those used to reinforce cement. He managed to grasp it with his left hand. Quietly he told Alma, "I'm turning on the furnace. Heat rises, right?"

"How do I know?" Alma said. "I've never been at the bottom of a barbecue before!" She turned to shield her head but moved too near the cage wall.

ROAR

Skull Face thrust its right arm into the top side of the cage. A series of welding joints gave way, and the monster's claws hooked into Alma's jacket. She screamed as the creature began to lift her entire body into the air and drag her closer.

"No!" Jackson cried out. He gave a last thrust at the gas valve with the metal rod, then swung the rod fast and hard at the creature's grisly arm. Its claws were locked on Alma's jacket as Jackson managed to pull her arms out of the sleeves. The beast shrieked, shredding the jacket like paper.

There were growls from another animal.

Alma recognized the sounds. "Coffin!" she cried out in the dark.

Jackson saw the huge, shaggy dog. Coffin had entered through the demolished window and plywood of the half-cellar wall, and lay crouched in the darkroom doorway. Teeth bared, he remembered his last encounter with the beast.

Alma heard the hiss and smelled the sickening sweetness of the gas as it discharged from the cluster of furnace jets.

"Scat, Coffin," Alma cried. The flames would light the windows, and even through the fog the soldiers would see the burst of light. They would come running and save them with their guns.

But something was wrong.

"The gas isn't lighting!" Jackson shouted.

"The pilot light must be out. You need a match."

"I don't have one."

"Then shut the valve off—or we'll all die!"

Jackson rolled onto his stomach, inched closer to the gate. He heard Skull Face scrambling on the cage above, saw the hideous arms and lethal claws hovering about the sides of the cage. Jackson looked for a discarded wood match on the floor, an old cigarette lighter—anything. The smell of the gas was stronger. He reached for the valve.

ROAR

Skull Face's hand swooped down, and Jackson recoiled. He felt a pain in his leg as though he had rolled onto a pen.

The piece of flint in his pocket.

The monster raged above him, both its arms now digging into the cage. A strip of welding gave way as Jackson grasped the triangle of flint. He pulled it from his pocket and struck up toward the rough metal of the gas jets. The stone hit and hit again, but there was no spark. He pulled Alma toward him as the creature's arms crashed down through the cage, scraping frantically.

Jackson thrust out the flint a third time.

There was a spark and a rapid whooshing sound. He saw the cloud of gas ignite, a dance of light that circled like a ghost, then settled onto the gas jets with the roar of a monstrous acetylene torch. Jackson saw the shock on the monster's face as the white heat whirled upward. Like a tick on a burning match cover, the monster sprang whole from the cage, landing against the far wall. It shrieked, its flesh on fire as it fled for the cellar door. With a single motion it burst the doors from their hinges.

Alma had felt the searing heat on her face and seen the burning. The rage of the fire was above them. She heard Coffin barking, saw him race after Skull Face. "Come back, Coffin!" she screamed. "Come back!"

Jackson pulled the goggles from his face and was the first one out of the furnace cage. He shut off the gas valve, then turned, reached out to Alma's grasping hands, and pulled her out after him.

Shadows and excited voices flew by the cellar windows. The soldiers were running, closing in. *Soldiers with guns*, Alma reminded herself. She ran to the cellar doors, scrambling up the steps. Jackson was fast behind her.

"Don't shoot!" Alma yelled, hoping the soldiers would hear. She wanted them to understand everything instantly, magically. That it was only she and Jackson. That it was Coffin chasing after the beast in the fog.

CRAAACK CRAAACK.

Two rifle shots.

Then silence.

Alma shuddered at the sight beyond the handful of young soldiers rushing to surround her. "No!" she cried as she pushed past them, running toward the heap of shaggy gray fur lying on the plain.

~11~
ESCAPE

D r. Cawley awoke from the heavy sedatives Dr. Nielsen and Sister Thornton-Sherwood had injected into her. She had been trapped in a nightmare, a horrid dream in which squirming, unearthly larvae were threatening to break out of a box no matter how tightly she held the lid shut.

When she opened her eyes, she realized she was in her hospital room. Her throat was dry and she was aware of a painful, raw sensation deep in her jaws. She tried to lift her hands to her face but couldn't. It took several moments more before she realized she was in a restraining harness.

"Nurse," she said. Her first words were an effort, but her mind seemed free of Ramid. Thoughts soon came clearly, seemed so completely her own that she considered the possibility that the army might have killed the monster. She raised her head and looked around the room, half expecting to see a guard.

She was alone.

An ugly green plastic pitcher of water sat on her bedstand. She tried to reach it, but her hands had only a few inches of leeway in the white cloth harnesses. She pulled gently to test the straps around the aluminum bed sides. They held.

The cord of the emergency signal had been pinned to a fold in the sheet near her hand. She pressed the button.

"What do you want?" came Sister Thornton-Sherwood's irritated voice over the room speaker.

"Water," Dr. Cawley said. "Please, may I have a drink of water?"

"When we have time."

"Please help me!"

"Shouting won't get us there any faster," Sister Thornton-Sherwood assured her.

"Please!"

Dr. Cawley heard the hum of the open speaker click off. She knew no one was listening any longer, that it was Sister Thornton-Sherwood's revenge. She thought about threatening the nurse, telling her she'd report her to Tillman and Rath, but logic told her the army must have given its approval for the harness. She pulled again on the bindings, knowing they were strong enough to restrain a gorilla.

There was a tearing sound.

At first Dr. Cawley thought she had torn the fragile material of her hospital gown. She glanced down to her left wrist and saw it was one of the straps that had torn. She tugged again, this time pulling both hands toward her chest.

The metal restrainers bent. Before they broke, the bindings ripped free.

Dr. Cawley realized she had become strong.

Very strong.

She swung her legs over the edge of the bed. Sitting up, she grabbed the water pitcher and drank. Too fast, she thought, as she felt cold drippings on her legs. Her mouth hurt as if she'd had major gum surgery. She raised her hands to her face and felt a painful swelling.

What is going on? she thought as she slid into her slippers and shuffled into the bathroom.

The image in the mirror took her breath away. Her lips and mouth were puffed up, as though someone had punched her. She moved closer, where the light from a fluorescent bulb was cruelly bright. If she'd fallen on her face, she'd stick it to Thornton-Sherwood and the hospital until they cried blood. She lifted her upper lip.

Her teeth looked okay.

She felt a rawness beneath her gums, and stretched

her lip higher. The gums were bleeding. She remembered her shouting. The invading thoughts intermittently controlling her were so powerful, they thrust her lower jaw forward as if straining to reshape her face into a muzzle.

"What are you doing out of bed?" came Sister Thornton-Sherwood's reprimanding voice behind her. "How did you get out of your harness?"

Dr. Cawley turned from the mirror to see a hypodermic needle poised. Reflexively, her lips stretched wide, grotesquely. Her jaws trembled with a new power, and she let out a rumbling growl.

Sister Thornton-Sherwood's mouth opened, tried to form a cry.

With instinctive speed and power Dr. Cawley clamped one hand over the nurse's mouth. With her other hand she relieved the nurse of the hypodermic and plunged its needle into her scraggly thin neck like a dart. Sister Thornton-Sherwood struggled violently in Dr. Cawley's grip, a silent, shaking bird, until she was asleep.

Dr. Cawley lifted Sister Thornton-Sherwood gently into her bed, quickly removed the white shoes and cap, and got her own coat from a tall metal cabinet. She put her makeup kit and radio into a shopping bag, left the room, and started down a set of fire stairs.

Nine flights down.

She found her paisley scarf in the coat pocket, wrapped it around her neck, and pulled it high to cloak her face. When she emerged from the stairwell, a guard held a paper cup at a coffee machine.

"Good night," Dr. Cawley said.

"Night," the guard said without looking up.

The wind was chilling as Dr. Cawley came out the main entrance. A solitary cab waited beneath the streetlight of a taxi stand. She headed for it. A young mustachioed driver wearing an earring interrupted his tea and cake, got out, and opened the door for her.

"Thank you," Dr. Cawley said, as she got into the backseat as ladylike as she could muster.

The driver got back behind the wheel, grunted, and threw open the glass partition. "Where to?"

"Salisbury," Dr. Cawley said. "As quickly as possible."

The driver laughed when he heard the accent. "You're from the States?"

"Yes," Dr. Cawley said.

"Well," he said, "it's different over here. Taxis don't take you a hundred kilometers whenever you feel like it. We say, 'Take the train.'"

Her thoughts began to fade and churn. The hostile power was taking control of her mind again and her jaw ached. Ramid's thinking of me, she told her-self. Ramid's come back into my head.

"Take me . . . to Salisbury," she repeated.

"You need a bus, lady." The driver took a bite of his cake.

Dr. Cawley trembled as she opened the door. She would try to hold on to her reason long enough to make the driver understand. She got out, stepped to his open window.

"You . . . take me," Dr. Cawley said.

"You're as sharp as a marble, you are," the driver said.

"Please. I need . . . your car."

The driver checked his watch.

Dr. Cawley sucked in air and let out a growl that rattled the cab. The driver looked up and saw the bes-tial expression on the woman's face. Dr. Cawley's lips were peeled back over her swollen, bleeding gums. She snapped her head back like a cobra, then thrust it for-ward into the driver's face.

The driver screamed, wet crumbs and coffee flying from his mouth. He jumped past his meter and out of the cab. Dr. Cawley got in behind the wheel. She threw the stick shift into first and floored the accelerator.

The driver was frozen in the middle of the street,

watching his cab travel away. He began to shiver and spin in shock.

"Help me!" he finally began to shout to the empty street. "Help me!"

~

Alma sat on the ground cradling Coffin in her arms while Jackson spun a story for Sergeant Keyes and his small team of terrified soldiers. They had heard the roar of the beast, seen the creature race off into the mist.

"Alma needed a book for her homework," Jackson told them. "Her father drove us out. He's coming back."

"You could have killed my dog," Alma blasted the soldiers as she held a cloth against Coffin's bleeding shoulder. Keyes was thrown by the accidental shooting of the wolfhound.

One soldier said, "You're lucky we showed up."

Alma felt like kicking him. "My dog needs a vet."

"Look, we've got problems," Keyes said, scratching his head.

Coffin staggered to his feet, dazed and bleeding, but alive. Alma stood with him, keeping pressure against his wound. "Dr. McGinn down the road is our vet."

"Take her," Jackson told Keyes.

Keyes thought a moment. "Okay." He signaled a young private to get a landrover.

Two other soldiers came up out of the cellar. "That ghoul thing trashed a window and part of a wall," one of them told Keyes.

The other soldier held the negative strip. "The kids were developing film."

"That's mine," Jackson said.

Keyes took the strip and held it up to one of the outdoor floodlights of the crematorium.

"All yours," Keyes said, offering the film.

Jackson took it, checked it. The chemicals had been on the film too long and destroyed all the images. He brought it over to Alma. "It's ruined," he said, trying to hide his smile. They both knew it meant that proof of the smaller hominids with the strange baby faces was gone. There'd be no way of Tillman or Rath knowing about them now.

The private drove up in the landrover. Sergeant Keyes went right onto the radio. A wind from the north was peeling the mist back toward the river. Soon, Jackson knew, the dune buggy would be in plain sight.

"I'm going to disappear," Jackson whispered to Alma.

"What?"

"They'll take you to the vet, then home to the close. Me they'd stick on a plane back to the U.S."

"What are you going to do?"

"I don't know," Jackson said. "All I *do* know is that I've got to help my aunt. I need to talk to her."

"Don't you realize it's no coincidence Skull Face showed up here tonight?" Alma said. "It didn't come back to the crematorium just because it's on a nostalgia trip."

"What are you saying?"

"This thing is building in power. It's going to go on a blood feast around here." Alma realized her voice was getting too loud; the soldiers were starting to stare. She dropped back into a desperate whisper. "Bullets don't kill it. Your aunt was the threat, as far as it was concerned."

"How could Skull Face know that?"

"The first army guy it killed—maybe it plugged into *his* brain, unloaded all he knew about your aunt heading up the search into the killings. Skull Face knew your aunt was the most dangerous one. It knew she was zeroing in on it."

"She did get Rath to follow the river."

"That night in the cemetery, it didn't just want to run by her and escape. The monster wanted to rip her to pieces. What he got was control of her brain."

Jackson petted Coffin's head gently. "I put you all in danger tonight."

"Look, Skull Face doesn't know much about me. If it can download your aunt's mind," Alma said, "it knows she drew the mural. It knows she showed it to you and told you about DOOM! DOOM! It's worried somebody's going to stumble onto something it doesn't want them to know."

Jackson nodded. "It knows everything she's been working on. The books, the sketches—all her research at the apartment. Her secrets."

"You're the one who's in a position to put it all together now. It knows that. Jackson, it's focused again. *You're the one it's stalking.*"

"You'll be safe at the close," Jackson said. He started to walk away.

Alma walked with him, keeping close by his side. "I want to go with you," she said.

"Take care of Coffin."

"You could wait for me," Alma said, putting her hands on her hips. "You need me."

"No," Jackson said. He backed away toward the wall of fog.

Alma was thankful Coffin's wound had stopped bleeding. She walked with Jackson, got him to circle so the soldiers would think they were merely helping Coffin get his gait back. Against the glare from the floodlights, Alma appeared to be a phantom; her hair had long shaken loose of its ponytail.

"I could check the old book in the cathedral library again," Alma said. "*In the Tomb Of the final Doom* must mean something."

Jackson said, "The 'Tomb' has got to be Stonehenge. Maybe you can find out more about the Doom Stone."

"I'll try. But you be careful," Alma said. "Don't do anything crazy. It's after you."

Jackson stepped back into the fog.

Alma continued to circle with Coffin back to the soldiers. No one missed Jackson until the buggy engine screamed from beyond the veil of the mist.

~ 12 ~
MOONRISE

Jackson kept the buggy on the dirt roads and easements running parallel to the A345 as he headed south. There were stretches of streetlight and a glow from frontage farmhouses. Fog continued to trace the banks of the Avon.

He was able to travel at a good clip on a shoulder road edging a farm, and took out the two-way radio. Please work, he thought, as he flicked on the power switch and tapped in 101, the code of his aunt's radio. There was static.

"Hello," Jackson said. There was another crackle of static, then a human sound of pain. "Aunt Sarah?"

More static. Then:

"Jackson?" His aunt's voice came over the receiver.

"It's me," Jackson said.

"Jackson . . ."

He heard a hum in the background like tires traveling fast on a macadam road. "Are you in a car?" he asked, surprised.

"I left . . . the hospital."

Her voice sounded fragile, anguished.

"The doctors said it was okay?" Jackson asked. "They said it was all right?"

There was a wheezing and a deep cry of agony. "What's happening?" he asked. "Where are you?"

The distress sounds became stronger but distorted in the receiver of the phone. Suddenly, Jackson had to swerve the dune buggy to avoid a defiant crow eating roadkill. It was picking at the carcass with its long, sharp beak, seemingly oblivious of the buggy bearing down on it.

There was a growling now from the phone, guttural sounds creeping lower.

Jackson said, "Tell me what to do, Aunt Sarah."

"The stone . . ." she said.

He remembered her rushing to the mural with her lipstick and rubbing it onto the top stone of the center trilithon. He could still see her placing her trembling hands into the crimson, dragging the color up high on the wall. "The one in your drawing?"

"Ramid is . . . afraid of the stone. . . ."

Jackson heard her fighting to get each word out. "Why is it afraid, Aunt Sarah?"

Her voice crawled lower into her chest again, snarling, grunting.

"He's . . . got me" came words, finally. "My mind . . ."

BZZZZZZ

Jackson heard the disconnect and was chilled. She sounded as if the monstrosity was at her side, its teeth at her throat.

He dialed her number again, let it ring until he heard a violent, ground-shaking roar coming fast from behind him, loud, powerful.

A tongue of fog from the river lay across the road and the parallel dirt path. There was a cluster of round barrows, mounds of the ancient dead, on his right.

He cut his lights and pulled the buggy in among them as an army convoy shattered the night. A communications lorry with a revolving satellite disk led the procession like an enormous cyclops. A pair of flatbed trucks hauled generators strapped to platforms.

Jackson ducked low on the seat as the caravan of vehicles flooded the road. The heart of the convoy was a slew of transports laden with armed troops, men sitting on benches facing each other under rippling canvas hoods. A van for top brass accelerated to pull in front of the convoy. It had walls of dark tinted glass and a massive, oversized air conditioner rising high from its rear.

Searchlights.

Jackson dropped into the ditch surrounding one of the mass graves. The lights cut like lasers over the top of the buggy.

Bringing up the rear of the convoy was a pair of huge tanker trucks with DANGER reflector signs. The trucks thundered past escorted by armed personnel in landrovers. One tanker was a high-octane fuel truck. The other's tank was longer, narrower, with complex gauges and steel wheel valves. The kind of truck that could carry extermination chemicals, poisons, Jackson thought.

Jackson was shaken as he climbed back onto the dune buggy. The sounds his aunt had made on the phone seemed no longer human. Why was she in a car? Where was she going? He didn't know whom he could turn to for help. The staff at the hospital thought she was hallucinating and mad—at best, belligerent. The army had no real reason to care about her except that she keep her mouth shut. She'd defined the beast, led them to it, and now they were caught up in the hunt. The convoy had to be on its way to supply the stalking teams out of Amesbury. They'd track Skull Face down to its lair this time.

His aunt had been right. The military was bringing in incendiary devices. Trucks with combustibles and poisonous gases that would certainly kill the small, innocent hominids. Even if the heavy artillery and chemicals were capable of doing what bullets couldn't, Skull Face would survive, Jackson knew. The monster would trick them. Escape through a secret tunnel. It would drift away in an underground river. Something cunning.

Ramid is afraid of the Stone.

He kick-started the buggy and headed south. The creature had been seared by the furnace. It would be raging home to lick its wounds.

Jackson couldn't worry any longer about staying on the easements and dirt roads. He set out across an open stretch of army training ground. There the sky was brushed clean of clouds, a black night stenciled with stars. Jackson saw a distant flickering of lights at the horizon to his left. It was advancing, and he knew it had to be the military search team moving westward and north with its weapons of death.

He wished Alma were with him. She would have been his voice of sanity.

Near Stonehenge he had to run the buggy near a private farmhouse in order to avoid the main entrance to Stonehenge with its chain-link fence. A corner of the crop field was a pear orchard with the older, weakest branches of its trees nailed to trellises. A pruning ladder lay in the grass near a well.

Jackson braked the buggy to a halt, shut off its motor and lights.

He knew he'd traveled faster than the beast. There would be time. He just didn't know how much.

He opened up the rear seat compartment, took out the loaded flare gun, and wedged it under his belt. He put the extra flare cartridges in his pocket, hung the radio by its strap around his shoulder, and set out on foot lugging the rickety, old wooden ladder.

Rabbits scurried in the weed cover as Jackson made his way past the earth ditches. He kept alert for open pits. A pair of horses feasted on the clipped grass nearer the stones. They were startled and shook the ground as they raced off frightened through the night.

Jackson shifted the weight of the ladder. The massive stones loomed as dark sentinels waiting for him, as he walked inside the circle to what was left of the horseshoe of trilithons.

He stopped in front of the trilithon his aunt Sarah had marked in her drawing. One of the uprights was gone, as well as the top stone—the one she'd streaked with red and about which she'd kept shouting *"Doom."* The crude, weathered ladder wasn't long enough to reach the top of the surviving upright.

He looked across to a stretch of four uprights with top stones that made up part of the main circle, and hauled the ladder over to them. He set it in place against an end stone. As he climbed, he felt dizzy.

On the last rung he took a deep breath and pulled himself onto one of the capping lintel stones. He grunted as he hauled the heavy ladder up after him.

The circle below was a black pit the stars could not light. He sat down on the lintel, took the radio hanging from his shoulder, and punched in his aunt's number. There was still no answer. It was possible she was hallucinating everything. It could be like voodoo. If she believed Skull Face's bite had power over her, then her mind could play tricks on itself.

The only thing Jackson was certain of was that the monster would have to be caught or killed. It was the only chance for everyone. His aunt Sarah. The people who lived around Salisbury Plain. If they got Skull Face in the open, the smaller hominids might be safe, because the army would call off the hunt and never know they existed.

Jackson ran his hands across the surface of the capping stone, felt the grooves that had been hand chiseled by human ancestors who had lived millennia before. Whose doom stone did his aunt believe it was? Not his. Even the outer circles were so high, there wasn't a chance Skull Face could reach him even if he showed up.

A scarlet glow began to form on the horizon. The

aura of red swelled, changing to purple, then orange. Finally, the glow became startling, and a huge ball of a moon lifted into the sky.

Jackson stood atop the stone. In the moonlight, the giant sarsen stones were a burnished crystal gray with faint streaks of yellow. They appeared to glow from within. The power of the full moon had always been a reality to Jackson. Hospitals reported more shootings and knifings during a full moon. Police departments knew more people went mad and murdered and robbed at full moon.

Is this your special moon, Skull Face? Jackson wondered. *The moon that comes back for you every nineteen years when it repeats its cycle? There must have always been a beast like Skull Face at Stonehenge. A lurking, hungry Minotaur.*

TICK

Jackson heard the creature, saw it moving toward him from an open field. He took the flare gun from his belt, checked the cartridge chamber, and held the gun ready. Skull Face had burns on its chest and legs, scars swiftly healing. The membrane of its face was blackened, pulled upward and taut to frame its demonic eyes.

The beast stopped a hundred yards from the stones, cocked its head to one side.

Jackson knew Skull Face was thinking.

TICK TICK

How much do you understand? it seemed to be wondering, measuring.

Jackson believed his aunt was right—the creature *was* afraid of this place. But the Doom Stone was gone. It was missing from the trilithons. There must be something else here, Jackson told himself. Something in front of my eyes that I'm not seeing.

An owl flew overhead, and for a moment Jackson remembered the life-size cement owls a lot of tenants in the high-rises of Manhattan use to keep pigeons away. Why would Skull Face be afraid of Stonehenge? Jackson asked himself.

Death.

From his perch he looked again at the shape of Stonehenge. The shadows from the rising moon were shifting quickly. A dark, long, thin cloud crept across the face of the moon. All of Stonehenge began to look like a giant jigsaw puzzle, its pieces shifting until Jackson realized what had been staring him in the face all along. The trilithons formed the shape of a skull, the shadows from the outer circle its jaw and teeth. In that moment he felt as if human ancestors, the people who built Stonehenge, were speaking to him from across five thousand years: *Only the Doom Stone can kill the monster.*

The creature moved closer, then stopped again. Jackson saw its eyes were still locked on him. He knew its brain was processing information. It could probably smell Jackson's fear. He guessed it was interpreting, evaluating his every move.

Jackson set the flare gun down, juggled the radio, and dialed again. There was the buzzing, then an open line and the hum of a speeding car.

"Aunt Sarah?" he said, not lifting his eyes from the beast.

He knew she was there, though she didn't speak. What if she was right about Skull Face?

"The monster's here," he said into the phone.

A new sound joined the hum from the racing tires. There was a shrill, rising cry like that from a tortured animal. It cut into Jackson's heart, and he knew time was running out.

"LET GO OF HER!" Jackson shouted across the field to Skull Face. The beast stepped backward, cracking twigs with its feet—then stopped again.

"Don't give up, Aunt Sarah," Jackson said into the phone. "I know about the Doom Stone. The creature's afraid of it because it can kill it."

Again the pathetic cry.

Furiously, Jackson picked up the flare gun, pointed it at Skull Face, and pulled the trigger. A thick, burning mass flew downward, whooshing in a fiery trajectory. It crashed into the ground to the right of the monster and bounced like a flat stone skimming a pond. Skull Face opened its glistening, fanged mouth and roared.

Jackson reloaded the gun. He was desperate to give his aunt even a shred of hope. The words flew out of him. "Alma's going to the cathedral. She found an inscription, a special book."

"You shouldn't have . . . told me" came his aunt's voice from the receiver. *Now Ramid knows.*

Jackson looked up quickly. Skull Face was gone. It had vanished from the field.

Tortured, bestial sounds erupted from the receiver—then a disconnect.

Jackson grabbed the ladder, lowered one end to the ground, and started down. He started to tremble as he realized where the creature was heading.

~13~

DOOMTIME

The veterinarian told Alma to leave Coffin with him overnight in the kennel. He explained to her, gently, that although the bullet wound was shallow, there would be drainage, and he needed to give the dog another round of shots in the morning. "He'll be as frisky as ever in a week. You can take him home tomorrow."

"You promise?"

"Yes."

Alma didn't mind leaving Coffin with Dr. McGinn. Coffin liked the doctor, and his ears shot straight up at the sight of a sleek Irish setter in the dog run next to his. Still, Coffin whined when Alma had to leave.

"Don't worry, boy," Alma said, rubbing his massive, shaggy head. "I'll be okay."

The young private was waiting in the landrover when Alma came out. He drove her south to Salisbury and pulled to a stop in front of the North

Gate. Alma thanked him for the lift home, got out, and headed across the grounds of the close. There were lights on in the cathedral. Alma knew it would be the Reverend Kalley working late on Saturday night. He always did a lot of the behind-the-scenes work to prepare for the Sunday services. He'd be doing everything from placing hymnals and offering envelopes in the pews to checking the condition of the choir robes.

The moonlight made the piping of the scaffolds creeping up the façade of the cathedral shine like a spiderweb. The scaffolding branched out along the sharp-angled slate of the main roof, then across onto the transepts. It made Alma dizzy to look up at the spire work platforms, where a construction elevator shaft rattled and creaked in the wind. Lesser pinnacles topped the bell tower itself, reaching up toward the night sky with the sharpness of spikes.

Alma entered the cathedral through the open door of the south transept. She felt safe inside its centuries-old medieval walls. She remembered the many times she had come into the sanctuary when there had been an organ playing and the voices of the choir drifted down from the balcony. She walked to the tiled base of the tower, where the children of the congregation had begun to build their annual Calvary display for Easter.

Beside it, under glass, was a detailed model showing the cathedral and the progress of its restoration.

"Reverend Kalley," Alma called up to the choir balcony.

"Hello?" came the cleric's deep voice. A moment later she saw his smiling bearded face peering down at her from the railing.

"It's me, Alma," she said.

"So it is. What are you doing up so late, young lady?"

"I wanted to look up something else in the cathedral library," Alma said. "May I?"

"Of course," the cleric said. "If you need help, let me know."

Alma was so worried for Jackson, she thought about telling the Reverend Kalley everything, but she had promised Jackson she wouldn't tell anyone. She simply said, "Thanks."

The cleric gave a wave and disappeared from the railing.

～

The entrance to the library was off the tower lobby, across from a faceless ancient clock. She opened the heavy oak door and went into the small musty room with its half-vaulted ceiling. Closing the door behind her, she flicked on a bank of fluorescent lights. The huge old parchment book on Stonehenge was on the shelf where she'd left it hours before.

Alma took the book and sat down at a reading table. She turned to the section about the monster and read again the riddle inscription that had been found on one particular stone from Stonehenge.

In the Tomb Of the final Doom. Alma read, her finger tracing each line in the old book, hoping she could find something to help Jackson. There were legends about wizards, and visions of dancing stones. Stonehenge was mentioned as having power over pestilence. The book said a single pebble from Stonehenge was enough to cure a well of a toad infestation.

She rubbed the goose bumps on her arms.

Finally she found a part Jackson would want to know. It told how the "Beast of Doom that walks at Stonehenge" could be killed only by a single sarsen stone which had been brought to Salisbury Cathedral centuries ago. "Where is the Doom Stone now?" Alma mumbled, speed-reading forward through the parchment pages. All she found was another riddle:

> *Doom Stone, tombstone*
> *In final repose,*
> *The longer it stands,*
> *The shorter it grows.*

But where *exactly* was it? She copied the riddle down on a piece of paper and slipped it into the pocket of her jeans.

THUMP

Alma heard the noise from above her. It was a dull, solid sound as if someone upstairs had dropped a heavy sack. She opened the door to listen. For a moment there was a delicate tinkling, like that from a metal wind chime. Then silence.

The silence became heavy, then jabbed at Alma like a stick in the ribs.

She left the library and went to the base of the tower again. "Reverend Kalley?" she called up to the choir balcony.

More silence.

"Hello, up there," she called louder. "Reverend Kalley, are you all right?"

Now the silence frightened her. She remembered a game the kids at school had played once about who had seen the most dead people. One kid had seen a train crash with two dead people. Another knew a family where three people died in a fire. Since living at the crematorium, Alma knew she'd win that game now hands down, though she didn't like the way her mind had turned to thoughts of death and bodies.

She started up the stairs of the tower. The balustrade

was thick and elaborately carved as it rose toward the shadowy choir loft.

"Reverend Kalley?" she called again, as she reached the second floor. The door to a storage room had been left open, and a line of hanging white choir robes swayed like headless ghosts in the breeze from an open window. A cluster of empty hangers began to make the tinkling sound again. What if the minister had passed out or had a heart attack? she thought. Several kids at her school had said they had seen or found people with heart attacks.

The wind from the window picked up, billowing the robes. Alma pushed her way among the flapping sleeves, trying to see if the cleric might have had an accident—perhaps fallen on the floor. The metal hangers clicked against each other, and she reached up to push them apart.

Alma first saw the feet and solitary dark robe. She lifted her gaze up through pleated whiteness to the form, saw the glistening red dripping down from the black frock, a terrible wetness making the fabric cling to a shape. Staring down at her was the Reverend Kalley hanging from a hook, his eyes frozen wide with only bone where the flesh of his neck had once been.

Alma screamed, and screamed again. She turned and struck out at the robes as they fluttered up to block her escape. She made it out of the room without falling. Now her cries reverberated in the vast space of the cathedral. She rushed toward the stairs but stopped fast at the terrifying sight waiting for her.

The monstrosity appeared to be smiling at her. It stroked the membrane furrowed on its brow. The hair on its body was singed, and what was left of it bristled up toward its neck. Several of its twisted teeth turned in upon themselves, were pronged to rip flesh wide.

She backed around the railing the only way she could go, toward the stairs that led higher into the tower. Moonlight crashed through a rosette of stained glass as the creature advanced. Its yellow and menacing eyes were locked onto Alma's face and thick mane of hair. The monster's cheekbones were covered with red, soiled like the face of a greedy child who'd eaten recklessly.

She started up the stairs with the monster after her. Her shrieks now formed into words. "Help! Oh, God, help me!" The solid and ancient stone of the cathedral, which had made her feel warm and safe, now smothered her sounds like a tomb. The wooden stairs narrowed as she went higher. The indoor scaffolding of the tower started at the third floor, and the monster swung out onto it. It grabbed the piping, rattled it like a toy, then climbed faster, swinging and roaring like a maddened primate after her as she raced higher.

Where is the Doom Stone? she found her mind screaming.

~

Jackson raced toward the close in the dune buggy. He was panicking, traveling too fast. The buggy almost flipped in a field of burrows. He'd traveled a long distance to a dead end in a farmer's high-fenced field. At one point he traveled too far west. Only the distant, moonlit spire of the cathedral pulled him back on course.

He couldn't think about what might happen if the creature reached Alma before him. He was frightened for his aunt—the ghastly animal sounds she had made on the phone. If she was driving back to Salisbury, she might go directly to Langford's. He considered stopping at the guest house, but he knew she'd know where he was headed.

Jackson pulled out the radio on a dirt road in Lower Woodford and turned on the power. When his aunt still didn't answer, he flipped frequencies.

"Can't anyone hear me? Can anyone hear?"

A man's voice came on.

"I need to talk to Sergeant Tillman," Jackson asked. "Can you get me to him?"

"No," the voice said bluntly.

"Tillman or Lieutenant Rath."

There was heavy static, then the voice came from the receiver. "They're airborne."

"It's an emergency. Can you call them?"

"Who is this?"

"Jackson Cawley. They know who I am. Tell them the creature they're looking for is heading for Salisbury Cathedral. Just tell them!" Jackson said. "Tell them!"

He had to hang up and grab the handlebar of the buggy with both hands as the dirt road became a jolting washboard. On an open field Jackson heard a throbbing clamor coming out of the south. An immense troop helicopter broke clear of a stretch of pines and swooped over him like a flashing spaceship. Instinctively, Jackson grabbed the flare pistol from his belt. He waited until the chopper was clear, then pulled the trigger. The flare traveled fast, hundreds of feet high into the air, and exploded at its apogee like a rocket. He knew if Tillman or Rath didn't get his phone message, whoever was on that helicopter would send them this one.

The chopper turned, began to circle the fire in the sky. Jackson kept his foot heavy on the accelerator. He managed to load the pistol with the third and final cartridge, and tucked it back under his belt.

He hit the town on North Castle Street.

When he reached the close, the sidewalks and grounds were deserted. The doors and windows of the brick and stone buildings and homes were closed tight. The only outdoor lights still burning were around the cathedral itself. Jackson braked the buggy to a halt. He slung the radio's strap over his shoulder, jumped off, and ran across the vast lawn.

The massive front doors of the cathedral were locked, their carved arches reaching high like weathered hands raised in prayer. But light spilled from the south transept, and he quickly ran to its entrance.

As he went inside, he heard the screams, cries from on high as from a tortured angel.

"Alma!" he shouted, tracking the sounds to the base of the tower. He looked up hundreds of feet into the air and saw her on the spiraling staircase of the spire. The monstrosity was closing in on her, thundering on the scaffolding.

Jackson summoned a cry that racked his body. "No!"

The creature stopped its climb, looked down to see Jackson racing two, three steps at a time up the tower steps.

"Save yourself," Alma cried out to Jackson.

The monster looked back up to Alma. Within

moments it could have been on her, its claws digging in to disembowel her high in the spire. Jackson watched it cock its head, twist its neck, insectlike, to stare back down at him. It was weighing information, considering a plan of action.

"The Doom Stone can kill it," Alma called to Jackson.

"I know."

"The book said it's here at the cathedral. The stone's here!"

"Where?"

"I don't know," Alma said.

Jackson called up to her, "Don't talk. It understands everything we say."

The creature roared, reached out, and shook the scaffolding violently. Several boards jiggled loose and fell hundreds of feet down to crash on the tower floor. The monster started down.

"Go back, Jackson. Go back!" Alma screamed.

Jackson got as high as the yoke level of the tower. Three rows of the cathedral's huge bronze bells hung between him and the creature as it lowered itself onto the opposite balcony.

He took the flare gun from his belt and held it ready. Again Skull Face roared, great currents of slime seeping down from the cavity that was its nose.

Alma's voice cracked as she called to Jackson. "There was another riddle in the book. I think it has something to do with where the Doom Stone is."

"Don't tell me," Jackson warned Alma, keeping his stare locked on the creature. "Don't even think about it."

The monster stood between him and the staircase that led up into the spire. It moved slowly around the platform, slices of moonlight falling through the vents of the bell tower and into the abyss between them.

TICK TICK

A maze of pipes and ducts was exposed from a section of the wall under reconstruction. One row of the giant bells, clappers poised, was held raised by a pulley system. The creature watched Jackson, saw him looking at the bells and the ropes. Jackson remembered the grimace on the creature's face when the engines on the chopper had roared in the cemetery.

"You don't like the noise, do you?" he asked Skull Face. "Other people's noise." He gave the pulley rope a sudden, hard tug, and the bells fell free.

The yoke creaked under the tons of moving weight. As each clapper hit the mouth of its bell, a deafening tolling began. The monster shrieked, appeared confused for a moment, but still blocked the stairs. Jackson shoved the flare gun back under his belt, grabbed a plank from the scaffolding, and threw it hard at the creature's feet. It jumped to one side.

Jackson raced up the stairs toward Alma, the radio bouncing against him on its shoulder strap. He heard the creature coming after him, rattling the pipes and boards of the scaffolding. Jackson pulled another plank loose, hurled it down at the creature. "It's still coming," Alma screamed. She followed Jackson's lead, began pulling planks loose from the pipe platforms. One of the boards hit the monster. It roared but kept on coming.

Jackson reached Alma on a platform seventy feet from the top of the spire. She was waiting with the paper upon which she'd copied the second riddle. There were chunks of discarded stone and broken tools on the platform. He pushed them off the edge. They cascaded down toward the creature, slowing its climb.

Jackson read the riddle quickly.

"We know there's a Doom Stone," Jackson said. "And we know that somehow it's supposed to kill Skull Face. But where's the stone? What does *The longer it stands, The shorter it grows* mean?"

Alma said, "Maybe it's part of the altar of the cathedral. Or the pinnacle."

"Let's hope it's the pinnacle," Jackson said, grabbing her and leading her up the stairs to the last platform of the spire. There was a small mason's table.

ROAR

The monster's arms flew up onto the platform, swinging its claws left, then right into corners like a bear raiding a rabbit's nest.

"Help me," Jackson said, grasping the table. They summoned up every ounce of their strength and pushed it over the edge of the stairs. It tumbled down, smashing hard onto the shoulders of the creature, then slid and fell more than three hundred feet to crash into the tile at the tower's base.

Jackson felt a draft.

The creature locked its claws on the platform and began to pull itself up to its prey.

Alma screamed, hit out at the beast with a plank, as Jackson ran his hands rapidly over the inner walls. He realized one section wasn't stone, only covered with weathering. He ripped the covering off. A small slab of the spire was a temporary aluminum plate. Moonlight cut in around its edges.

Jackson kicked and the metal plate flew open. The top of the outside scaffolding ring lay shifting in the wind.

"Go!" he shouted, pushing Alma through the narrow opening. At first she felt only the planking beneath her feet swaying from the suspension ropes. Jackson was out after her, knowing the slit would be too narrow for the monster.

The creature's claws shot out through the small hole. Jackson grabbed Alma's hand, pulled her after him toward the perimeter of the platform.

At first Alma was disoriented. When she looked down, she saw lights going on in several of the buildings of the close. It was a dollhouse village, she thought, until the reality of the perspective, that they were some three hundred feet below her, clutched suddenly, violently at her throat.

She began to scream, backing away from the edge.

"What's the matter?" Jackson asked.

"It's *high!*"

"Of course it's high." Jackson kept them moving away from the creature's thrusts and the hole in the spire. He held tight to Alma's hand, moved around the platform, keeping close to its center. "Look up at the pinnacle," Jackson said as a cold night wind struck them. "Is it gray with yellow streaks? Is it the Doom Stone?"

The wind snapped Alma's hair as she held tight to Jackson and looked up.

"No," she said. "It's white with curlicues, like cement that was poured into a mold."

Through cracks in the planking Jackson saw two

other platforms below them suspended by ropes. "Can you climb down the ropes to the next platform?"

"Are you crazy?"

"You've got to try."

Alma backed closer to the spire. "Where's the creature?"

Suddenly there was a great crash behind her. The arm of the beast thrust through the stone wall of the spire a foot from her head. Alma was thrown forward toward the edge of the platform. She saw the whole of the drop below as she went over the edge, but Jackson grabbed her hand. The weight of her body pulled him toward the drop with her. She dangled, screaming, "Don't let me fall! Don't!"

Jackson began to slide, helpless, his body inching to the edge. He tried to dig his feet into the planking, held his hand out to push against one of the suspension ropes. He heard the crashing of the stones behind him, turned to see the monster had opened the side of the spire wide and was coming out onto the platform after him.

Jackson began to swing Alma.

"No!" she yelled.

It took her a moment before she understood he was making a pendulum of her. As the monster roared and loped out at Jackson, he let go of Alma.

She landed on the platform below as he grabbed the suspension rope and threw himself after her head-first.

Below, people had heard Alma's screams and begun to come out of their homes. Others ran down St. John Street toward the cathedral. Jackson eased back from the edge, with the creature on the platform above them.

"Don't make a sound," Jackson whispered to Alma, but she was too panicked. She started to crawl around the platform looking for a way down. The boards creaked, signaling her position.

CRASH

The planking above their heads exploded, and the inverted torso of the monstrosity dropped down at them. Jackson rolled, pulled Alma after him as Skull Face let loose a loud, shrieking blast. It righted itself as it landed.

Jackson's fingers dug into a loose wide plank.

"Help me," he yelled to Alma.

Together they pried it up. Alma dropped down through the hole to the last level of the spire's scaffolding. Jackson was right after her. The final platform was more solid, attached to the sturdy pipe scaffolding of the main tower. Alma saw crude plank stairs and started down as fast as she could go, Jackson right behind her.

They passed a dozen subpinnacles that sprang from the summit like huge, intricately carved daggers.

Jackson asked, "Are any of them sarsen stone?"

"No."

Alma was so busy checking the stones of the tower, she didn't notice the stairs came to a dead end at roof level. "Watch out!" Jackson shouted as she stepped off into air. She managed to grab the side of the scaffolding. In a second he had a grip on her and pulled her back onto the planking. From the roof it was a ten-story drop to the ground.

ROAR

The creature was coming fast down the scaffolding. A narrow catwalk led out along the rim of the sharp-angled roof.

"Let's go," Jackson said, dragging her behind him along the catwalk. It ended more than sixty feet out along the edge. There was a wide gap of open roof before the scaffolding resumed at the back of the cathedral.

"If we can make it to the elevator shaft, we'll be home free," Jackson said.

Alma saw the creature drop onto the roof level. She turned to Jackson. "What do we do now?"

"Come on." Jackson climbed off the catwalk onto the steep slant of the lead-and-tile roof. He lay flat, his legs stretched out toward the roof gutter, hoping to prevent a slide. He began moving sideways like a crab.

"Hurry!" he urged Alma.

She watched him dig his fingernails into the lead casings—saw him search out toeholds on the chiseled surface of the tiles. None of it looked very secure.

She looked again to Skull Face, as the monster headed out onto the catwalk. She felt herself shaking, could barely breathe. *Please let us be okay,* she kept saying to herself.

"I'm coming," she called to Jackson.

She climbed over the end of the catwalk and lay on her stomach as she followed him. Her nails clawed into the lead. The tiles were cold against her face. *Clink! Clink!* She heard the tiles jiggle beneath her. Jackson saw her terrified face. He wanted to comfort her, to say everything was going to be fine, but he wasn't certain of that at all. He moved closer to the elevator shaft.

"Jackson," he suddenly heard her call in a strange excited whisper.

He planted his fingertips into a firm grip on a casing before looking back. He saw her staring at the roof, moving her hands over the tiles as though they were encrusted with gemstones.

"What?" he asked.

"The tiles . . . the roof tiles . . ." She lifted her gaze, let it drift upward toward the top of the roof. "They're sarsen stone."

Jackson looked at a single tile, past its silvery frame of lead. He recognized the crystal gray and faint streaks of yellow, and knew she was right. "We're *lying* on the Doom Stone?"

Alma whispered, "*The longer it stands, The shorter it grows.* That's the answer to the riddle: The Doom Stone's been cut into *tiles!*"

ROAR

Jackson's concentration was shattered. The flare gun had worked itself out of his belt, began to slide noisily down the roof. *Oh, no,* he thought as he watched it fall over the edge and disappear. He himself began to slip down the sharp pitch of the roof. For a moment the shoulder strap from the radio caught the edge of a casing, but then it slipped free. Alma reached out to stop him. She began to slip, too.

"Ahhhhhh!" Jackson cried out as his feet hit the gutter. It snapped under his weight. She saw him slide over the edge and out of sight.

She heard him gasping.

Alma stopped her slide. Carefully, she inched down and peered over the edge of the roof. Jackson was clinging to a piece of tin gutter that had ripped, been bent down.

The tiles beneath her were cracking, moving as if they were alive. She searched for a grip, dug her fingers in deeply.

CRACKKKKK . . .

A single tile sprang loose, slid past her, and dropped the more than a hundred feet down to crash onto a sundial in a rock garden.

Finally, her grip held.

"Grab me," she yelled.

Jackson reached up, took her hand. She squeezed her eyes shut and pulled slowly, steadily. When she opened her eyes again, she saw she was helping him shimmy up the twisted section of the gutter and back onto the roof. The creature was at the end of the catwalk, watching.

"Don't look at the tiles," Jackson whispered as he moved faster toward the rear scaffolding and wire mesh of the elevator shaft. "It's reading our body language. We need it to move out onto the tiles."

"Why?"

"Who knows if that's how the Doom Stone works? Maybe it has to be on it, on the tiles."

"But it's been cut up—the Stone could have lost its power."

Jackson reached the rear scaffolding and pulled himself up onto the platform around the elevator shaft. He locked his hand in Alma's and helped her climb up next to him. He hit the call button for the elevator cage, but it remained dead at the bottom of the shaft.

"What's wrong?" Alma asked.

"The power switch must be on ground level."

Suddenly a band of floodlights illuminated all the cathedral grounds. Eyes of headlights converged on the close like lions racing in for a kill.

"They're here," Jackson said. "Soldiers are here."

The creature saw the activity below. It raised its head, moving mantislike to look at Jackson and Alma, then at the tiles on the roof.

It's thinking too much, Jackson worried.

He glanced back down to the ground. A check-ered white-and-red taxi drove recklessly into the close and across the lawn until it reached the wall of military vehicles. He recognized the driver when she got out. The woman pressed a radio to her ear.

"It's my aunt," Jackson told Alma.

Dr. Cawley stared up at them. Jackson took his own radio from his shoulder strap and flicked it on.

"What are you doing?" Alma asked.

The creature roared again, its eyes scanning the roof.

"Skull Face is wondering about the tiles," Jackson said. "We've got to change its mind."

"How?"

There was a crackle of static from the radio. Jackson knew the line was open. "Aunt Sarah?"

An animal growling came from the radio. "Aunt Sarah, we found the Doom Stone," Jackson said.

"I thought you said telling her is like telling Skull Face," Alma said. "It'll read her mind."

Jackson covered the mouthpiece. "That's why I've got to tell her a *lie*," he shot at Alma. Back into the receiver, he said, "Aunt Sarah, the Doom Stone's in the cathedral. It's behind the altar."

He saw his aunt start away from the taxi and head for the entrance.

The creature reacted, swiveled its head like a radar dish, then locked its eyes on Jackson and Alma. It climbed over the edge of the catwalk and started across the roof toward them.

"It's coming!" Alma screamed.

"Distract it!"

"How?"

"Make faces. Stand on your head. Anything!"

"I can't!"

"Do *something!*"

The creature reached the middle of the roof and

was closing on Jackson and Alma. It looked confident that the tiles were no threat, that there would be nothing between it and the prey it needed to kill. Jackson tried to get his aunt back on the radio. She disappeared under the eave.

All Alma could think of doing to confuse it was sing. She let out a few notes, her mind racing to think of any song she knew. She remembered her mother's favorite song, one they used to sing together on karaoke nights. She'd also sung it with the school chorus. "*My wild Irish Rose . . .*" she found the words slipping out of her trembling throat, "*The sweetest flower that grows . . .*"

The creature stopped.

Alma could see the bafflement in its eyes.

"Keep singing," Jackson said.

"I feel like a fool."

"But a *live* fool."

Alma started the song again; this time her hauntingly beautiful voice sailed across the roof. "*My wild Irish Rose . . . the sweetest flower that grows . . . la la la dee da dum . . . la la la dee da dum . . .*"

Skull Face locked its eyes on Alma, as Jackson turned his back. "Ot-nay rue-tay!" Jackson whispered into the radio. "E-thay oom-Day tone-Say is-ay up-ay on-ay e-thay oof-ray!"

"What are you doing?"

"Skull Face may be too freaked by your singing to read my aunt's mind. If it can, it's going to have to understand pig Latin. *Sing!*"

There were scraping sounds as the tiles under the creature's feet began to loosen. *Fall, fall,* Jackson wished silently. Skull Face sensed the danger now, sprang quickly up to the top of the pitch. The tiles of the ridge held firm, and the creature crossed toward the back of the church to the ridge above them.

Alma sang louder, dread creeping into her voice as the creature started down for them. There was a pulsing thunder as a trio of helicopters roared over a ridge to the north.

"It's got to be Rath and Tillman," Jackson said. "They'll call off the search. They won't find the flint mines. The little hominids will be safe."

"But they're too late for us," Alma cried.

Jackson put down the radio and turned with her to face the monstrosity. They backed against the wire mesh of the shaft. The creature was on them, roaring, raising its ghastly arms. Its appalling fluids oozed from between its teeth, two thick streams bursting from the mouth and spilling over its chin.

Jackson shouldered himself in front of Alma as the creature's claws reached out. It was then he felt the shaft of the elevator vibrate. The cage below had come alive and was traveling up toward them.

"Sing with me," Jackson said, and he launched into the song, at the top of his lungs:

"MY WILD IRISH ROSE . . . THE SWEETEST FLOWER THAT GROWS! LA LA LA DEE DA DA . . ."

Alma joined him.

Skull Face moved its face close to theirs, dissecting them with its eyes, sniffing at them.

Suddenly, the head of a figure loomed behind them. Jackson turned, saw his aunt and what she held in her hand. He pulled Alma to the side as the safety door was flung open. Dr. Cawley held the flare gun. She pulled the trigger. A ball of white fire roared out at the creature.

The fireball caught Skull Face in the stomach, pushing it back out onto the roof. The flames took root and began to crawl quickly up its chest to engulf its head.

Shots rang out from one of the circling helicopters. One. Two. Three.

The monster shuddered. It tottered to the edge of the roof, then fell downward like a grotesque rag doll. Alma, Jackson, and his aunt watched its long plunge toward the rock garden. There was a quick, sudden, and sickening cracking of bone as the spike of the sundial tore up through the monster's body.

Dr. Cawley put her arms around Jackson and Alma, turning them away into the elevator. "Are you all right?" she asked.

Jackson looked into her eyes. He saw she had returned from wherever the power of the monster had taken her.

Scraping sounds.

"Look," Alma cried, pointing to the roof.

The tiles had begun to fall, to slide and drop. They rained quickly, savagely, like deadly blades, down upon the creature until its body was blanketed in a great mound of shattered silent stone.

EPILOGUE
MADAGASCAR—ONE YEAR LATER

Dr. Cawley felt the happiest she'd been in a long while as she drove along the coast of Madagascar heading for the airport. She hadn't seen Jackson since the events at Stonehenge. They'd written a great deal, compared each others' nightmares. By now they had almost begun to believe the story as the army had wanted them to tell it: The bad dream at Stonehenge had been completely explainable by a series of unfortunate events. A pet bear had turned savage, escaped from a private estate, and done the killings. The creature seen by so many atop the cathedral was someone in a masquerade costume, a man who had flipped out on drugs. Anything else was some sort of mass hallucination. Every aspect of the horror had been methodically cleansed by the military press machine, expert in manipulating rumors and transforming truth.

All the charade was worth it, Dr. Cawley, Jackson, and Alma had agreed. The existence of the other hominids was something they knew must be kept to themselves for a time, or they would not have gone along with it. In a few short months—in summer—it would be safe to quietly return to Stonehenge and explore the secret only they knew still breathed and moved and waited for them.

Dr. Cawley was happy Alma's father had let her accept the invitation to join her and Jackson for their spring break. Jackson was to be on the three-P.M. flight from Kennedy; Alma would be arriving on the four ten P.M. from Heathrow. The dig itself in Madagascar wouldn't be very exciting, but she had so many wonderful things to show them on the island. The farmers and herders were friendly. Jackson would want to search for treasure left by Captain Kidd and the hordes of other sea pirates who had once plundered off the coast. The lightning storms were spectacular. They'd visit the coffee and sugar plantations, the vanilla and oar factories.

She could already hear Jackson's voice in her mind.

"Stop the car! Stop the car!" he'd cry out.

She knew he'd be jumping out of the car to pet the sheep and goats. He'd want to ride a horse. To fish. Sail. And he'd ask so many questions.

Most of all, she knew Jackson and Alma would

spend hours on her favorite dock near the dig. Giant manta rays would rise to look at them and then curl magnificently to reveal their massive white bellies. At night Dr. Cawley would show the kids how to snatch handfuls of plankton, rub them, and make their hands explode with brilliant, shocking luminescence.

As Dr. Cawley drove to the airport, there was no way she could know what was happening deep in the ground thousands of miles away. In the blackness of the flint mines beneath Salisbury Plain, one pale face and body had begun to transform, to move and sound and appear different from the other living forms around it. It knew its limbs were growing faster, stronger. Its skull had become larger, its hunger grown beyond the small, brittle, and mucoid forms that crawled at its feet. It had been a while now since it had learned to crawl from time to time up the long distance to the surface. It was drawn to find a hole that looked up toward the starry nights. There it found rodents and other small animals that strayed across its path. It used the sharp, growing daggers that were its teeth. It feasted and dreamed, waiting for the return of its special moon.